Blessed Lands
Egypt

J Carrell Jones

Mythical Legends Publishing

A Mythical Legends Publishing Trade Paperback Original

Copyright © 2011 by J Carrell Jones
Published by Mythical Legends, 2013
Publisher@mythicallegends.com
http://mythicallegends.com

ISBN 978-0-9627835-9-3
Library of Congress Control Number: 2013912375

Printed in the United States of America

9 8 7 6 5 4 3 2 1

DEDICATION

To my brilliant and beautiful daughter Nicholette, you are the future.

J CARRELL JONES

ACKNOWLEDGMENTS

Google, You make me look like a genius!
Wikipedia, Everyone who contributes to the World Brain –
Thanks! You are appreciated.
The Papyrus Ani (or the Book of the Dead) -
http://www.masseiana.org/
A Concise Guide to Ancient Egypt's Magic & Religion (Kindle
Edition) by Maria Isabel Pita
Egyptian Tales Translated from The Papyrus (Kindle Edition),
edited by W. M. Flinders Petrie
The Egyptian Book of the Dead (Kindle Edition) by K. A. Wallis
Budge

J CARRELL JONES

Preface

Ayruyi looked up with tears in her eyes. She saw the miracle. Her master healed Akila in witness to her eyes. She repositioned herself and knelt in front of Honute. "Oh, Master Honute, Healing Priest, I bow to you my humble form and give you my life. I witnessed the miracle of power and you are my living god, the embodiment of Ra, Horus, Osiris, Pharaoh." She started giggling. It was slow and soft, then built up to a frightening hysteria of laughter. She tore her clothes off in a crazed possessed way and rubbed Akila's blood over her body. She screamed out, "I am witness to a new god. Glory be to the mighty Master Honute. Honute-Ra I say! Honute-Ra!"

Honute was horrified. He grabbed at Ayruyi's thrashing body as it tried to cover itself in blood.

She screamed again. "Honute-Ra! Honute-Ra! I am your slave. Command me." She laughed wildly and embraced Honute in a passionate hold. She sobbed and laughed and giggled and moaned and rubbed herself against him. She screamed out loud again as she reached an orgasm. Its intensity enveloped her in a crash of intense convulsions. It peaked within seconds and she blacked out.

Honute sat there holding a passed out Ayruyi, who was moaning and giddy at the same time.

Akila knelt beside him. "Is she all right?"

He nodded. Then the realization hit him. Ayruyi's reaction may not be so unusual. Suppose others react the same way. His mind raced and he felt dizzy. "Oh Thoth, what have you done!"

Akila looked at Honute and said, "What do you mean?"

He placed his blood covered hand to his forehead. "All is lost. They're going to treat me like a god. This is going to be a curse."

Then it hit Akila. Honute was right. The other shoe just dropped.

Prologue

The Oracle swayed back and forth chanting a litany from the book of Vision. Smoke padded the floor like a thick carpet. At its surface the wispy licks moved like tormented snakes. The room smelled of cedar, the way the Oracle liked it. There was no reason for the smoke, but it made for great drama and tension. The Head Priest of the Middle Lands, Vizier of the Area for Pharaoh, Friend to the Royal Family, stood at the door way impatiently. The Oracle motioned for the Priest to move closer. She was ready to give him some information. "Enter my chamber, O'mighty Priest of the Middle Lands. I have what you requested."

Ferruk-amon Islat Huytrep-Ra stepped through the threshold. He had waited for this audience nearly a month. The old woman knelt in the smoke filled room chanting gibberish. She was swaying back and forth, eyes unfocused and staring at a smoke covered wall. He asked, "You have seen?"

The Oracle turned to Ferruk and nodded. "I have seen."

"Tell me then. What of the future?"

"Have you made the proper arrangements?"

Ferruk was nearly beside himself. The old bag was talking about money when he wanted an answer. "Yes, as usual. When have I faulted on our agreements?"

The Oracle chuckled. The noise filled the chamber with eerie echoes of her haunted sound. "Then come closer and gaze into my bowl."

Ferruk stepped close to the Oracle. A large iron bowl sat in front of her.

He peered into the bowl with its simmering pool of liquid. Colors swirled in a multitude of different hues, shifting from one color to another. Ferruk stared closer and he saw a man in modest priestly robes poised in a stance that reminded him of a fight. His hands aglow in blue light growing brighter and brighter until the light flashed in brilliance that nearly blinded him.

Ferruk wiped his eyes, clearing the spots before him. Then the image was gone and the colors within the liquid disappeared.

"Who is this man?" Ferruk said.

The Oracle stood up and walked to an open door opposite the room. "I am tired now. Please leave."

Ferruk blocked her way, anger boiling over as he tried to stare her down.

"Do you treat Pharaoh this way?"

The Oracle laughed at this posturing. "Mighty Priest, this man will be your undoing."

"What do you mean? Tell me! I command you!"

"You are not Pharaoh." The Oracle stared back and Ferruk lost his breath.

He stepped back and to the side. His eyes dropped.

She walked to the threshold and stopped. "Head Priest of the Middle Lands, Vizier of the Area for Pharaoh, Friend to the Royal Family, he will kill you."

"Impossible!" Ferruk said with so much intensity that he nearly startled himself.

The Oracle chuckled as she walked through the opened doorway. "It is possible. Come see me tomorrow and I will give you more information. I am tired now and the vision fades." She closed the door.

Ferruk stood there listening to the old crone's laughter in the distance. It echoed throughout the chamber and seemed to slap him with a cruel and taunting threat, '. . . he will kill you.'

Honute had just stepped out of the temple when it happened. It was like no other. Time crawled and a moment seemed to never arrive. The streets of New Heliopolis erupted in a scream of gun fire and screeching tires. Honute turned to the sound and saw a car slide into a turn some one hundred feet away. The driver yanked the wheel right, then left. The car swished along the tarred streets trying to grip the roadway. At the end of the path were two children. Honute slipped out of his sandals and prayed to Thoth for the strength to do what he had to do. He lifted the bottom of his priestly robe and sprinted the impossibly long distance in an impossibly short amount of time. He grabbed the kids, each in one arm, twisted his body, and lifted his legs up. The driver stumped on the brakes and skidded to a halt. Honute hunched his back and said, "Thoth help us," as the windshield slammed square center. Honute and the kids bounced off. Screams merged with the crash of metal and glass. The car a wreck and the windshield pushed in. The kids saved and Honute standing there unharmed. A man emerged from the car and lunged at Honute. Decades of honed skill snapped into play and muscles worked autonomously. Honute was a passenger in a body that reacted immediately with devastating force to an immediate threat. The danger had been neutralized. The man lay on the ground, subdued.

The police arrived soon after and arrested the man. A grateful mother ran to the kids and hugged them in her arms. She wept and smothered them with kisses. One kid said, "Mom, did you see us fly in the air?" The other one said, "Wee, what a ride!"

The Mom stood up and faced Honute. "Thank you, sir, thank you."

Honute smiled and said, "Call me Honute. And you are welcome. Thoth gave me the strength to help."

She squatted back down and showered the kids with more kisses and hugs. She looked up and asked, "What can I do to repay you? Sir . . . Priest Honute?"

"Just Honute," He replied.

"There has to be something? Please?"

Honute smiled and said, "I know times are hard, but a small offering and a prayer to the modest temple of Thoth would do nicely."

The woman looked around and spotted the temple a hundred

feet away. She looked at Honute then back to the temple. The deity Thoth must be very powerful to have enabled this priest to travel the equal distance of the car to save her two kids. She kissed them again and nodded to Honute. "I will make an offering. Thoth is most powerful."

Honute smiled and continued on his way to the market. His sister, Honuti, received a promotion and he wanted to prepare a special meal for the occasion. Despite problems at home Thoth was good to him these days.

Chapter 1

The doorbell rang. Honute was expecting his twin sister Honuti. She sounded excited over the phone. "Take a deep breath and tell me." He told her. She inhaled a deep breathe, held it for a few seconds and let it out in one big rush of air. "I got promoted." She said. Honute, blinked a few times. "Really?"

"Yes." She replied.

"This is wonderful news. We'll celebrate tonight. Bring Anumetus."

The doorbell rang again. Honute stepped out of the kitchen. "I'll get it." He said to no one in particular and stepped the short distance to the door. Their apartment, Hypatia and Honute, was modest. It wasn't as large as some of their friend's. His position as a local priest brought home a decent check. It was Hypatia who was the bread winner of the family. Her salary was nearly twice that of his meager pay. His check paid the bills and living expenses. Her check paid for the apartment. Honute looked through the peep hole and saw his twin. He opened the door, "Honuti!" He gave her a big hug. The last time she came over for dinner was about six months ago. The evening had been pleasant enough in the beginning then Hypatia had had a little bit too much to drink. The same old resentment bubbled up to the surface and they argued about the old issues.

"Come in, come in." He said.

Honuti stepped in and handed him a bottle of date wine. He took it and patted Anumetus on the back. Anumetus nodded and smiled amiably. He was a quiet decent looking guy. His hair was jet black and his skin was olive brown. Honuti complimented him by being almost pale white. Honute smiled at the vast differences between the two. He was tall and dark, she was Honute's height with very fair skin. Her hair was a flowing brown when it wasn't tied up in a ponytail. Honute looked at his own complexion. He was several shades darker than his twin, but his was the result of being out in the sun giving blessings to pilgrims and local worshipers. "Dinner will be ready in about thirty minutes." Honute took the wine into the kitchen and found a corkscrew. He popped the cork and poured three glasses. He sniffed the air and turned to the oven. Several game hens baked golden brown were nearly done. He took a cooking brush, dipped the head into a jar of butter oil and wiped each bird until the skin was shiny. A clear pot of mixed vegetables boiled silently. He lifted the lid and tipped in a little bit of salt. The air filled with the smell of carrots, cabbage, and peas. The second pot was bubbly and spat out a smooth flour gravy sauce. It hit the counter in a wet splat. Honute grabbed a cloth and wiped the spot up. He dropped in some whole black mushrooms and stirred until the mushrooms disappeared. The mushrooms had been declared out of season, but Lucutus, the store owner grew them in the store basement. They were a gift. Honute had blessed his store, for free, when Lucutus thought he run into bad fortune and told Honute that he could not pay him much. Creditors and the regional Vizier visited that afternoon. Lucutus said that he tried praying to Bes, but he believed his prayers fell on deaf ears and so needed a priest. A few weeks after Honute blessed the store Lucutus came into an inheritance from a nearly forgotten relative. To show his appreciation Lucutus told Honute that he can have up to two pounds of anything in the store, each week, for the rest of his life. Hypatia had been furious when she learned that Honute performed the ritual for free. She screamed, yelled, and threw things across the room. She had fumed for several days until Honute brought home two pounds of Royal Honey. He told her it was a gift. She didn't believe him and promptly checked the credit cards and bank account for recent transactions. Royal Honey sold for $100.00 an ounce. She pressed

Honute further for the truth. He said Lucutus gave it to him to show his appreciation. She blinked several times and stared at him in silence. He shrugged and suggested he would take it back if she wasn't happy with the honey. She continued to stare in silence. After a few moments, Honute repacked the Honey and left. An hour later he returned with two pounds of lamb and dates and cooked dinner. The two sat in total silence chewing and swallowing. Occasionally the deafening absence of sound was cut by the contact of metal utensils against ceramic plates. After dinner, Honute cleaned up and washed the dishes. He went into one of the rooms that had been converted into an office. Both had their own office – it was an easy arrangement the two made. Several hours later Hypatia tapped lightly on the door. She stepped in and asked how much did the lamb and dates cost. She was balancing the book and needed to make an entry. He looked up from reading and said, "It cost nothing. It was a gift," and buried his nose back into his prayer book. Hypatia tried to conceal the pained look on her face as she closed the door. Realization hit her hard at what Honute had traded in exchange for the Royal Honey. And that was pretty much how their life went.

Honute walked out the kitchen with the three glasses in his hands.

Honuti took two and gave one to Anumetus, "To success and prosperity." She said.

Honute looked up when he heard keys in the front door. He crossed the path to greet Hypatia. The door opened and he saw his wife was in a foul mood.

Hypatia noticed Honuti and Anumetus standing in the living room holding glasses of wine. She said, "What are you doing here?"

Honuti reacted to the indignity and was about to reply when Honute said, "Remember Hyp, I left you a message on your voice mail at school."

Hypatia glared at Honute.

"Honuti got promoted and we are celebrating. I cooked us a

nice dinner."

Hypatia blinked a few times. Her jaw muscled worked silently. "Congratulations. Maybe it's a good thing that one of you is ambitious."

Honute cleared his throat. "How about we have a nice evening. This is something special."

Hypatia responded, "I'm not hungry. I ate something earlier and I feel tired. You guys enjoy yourselves." She headed for the bedroom.

Honute watched her in stunned silence as she walked down the hall and slammed the door shut. He looked at his twin and her fiance. He let out a deep sigh and shrugged. "I'm sorry, Honu. I don't know what's gotten into her. Lately, she's been in a bad mood."

Honuti drained her glass and sat on the couch.

Anumetus sipped at his and sat. For the moment he decided to remain quiet.

"Nute," Honuti began, "Don't worry about it. She just had a bad day."

The group was silent for a bit. Honute sighed. "Maybe we should celebrate another time."

Honuti smiled slightly. She figured her brother wanted to talk to Hypatia. She nodded, gave Honute a kiss on the cheek and collected Anumetus for their departure.

Honute stood on the balcony looking out over the city. It was late and most of the city lights were out. The air was clear and smelled of recent rain fall. The streets were slick and had a shiny appearance in the late night. Hypatia was asleep in their bedroom. After Honuti and Anumetus left, Honute, determined to find out once and for all what was wrong with his wife, stormed through the doorway to their bedroom. Hypatia was still in her work clothes – white linen sheet folded and wrapped around her body and sandals still on her feet – was sound asleep. It wasn't that he didn't love his wife or that she didn't love him, it was that they hardly saw each other. She was head lecturer and astronomer at the University of New Heliopolis, Great Temple of Amon-Ra. Her workload tripled when the previous head lecturer, Dr. Turtukilo took another post at the Serapis Institute of Technology, Lower House of the Temple of Ptah. So, like all the other nights, Hypatia would drag herself into the apartment, walk into the kitchen to grab a bottle of Honey ale and sit and vegetate. She would mutter something about the school looking to hire more help. Same thing every night, except this night. She insulted his sister and embarrassed herself. Honute unwrapped the cloth around Hypatia and placed it in the laundry basket. He placed her shoes by the bedside and drew the covers and tucked his wife in. Just before he left he kissed her on the forehead and blessed the room. He mumbled a long memorized prayer. He prayed to Isis and asked her to help him and Hypatia find their happiness.

Chapter 2

Dr. Theoris ran the simulation again. She pushed her dull dark gray framed glasses high up on the bridge of her nose. The glasses were a gift. Her father gave them to her when she received her first Ph. D. That was twenty years ago. They bothered her then and they bothered her now.

The computer predicted that the two atoms would behave as one. "Akila, could you get me the data on the Entangle Range?"

"Yes, Doctor." Akila had been Dr. Theoris' assistant for five years. Akila was working toward a Doctorate in Magickal Manifestation. Theoris had been the leader of Manifestation investigation for the last decade. No one in the Blessed world could match her accomplishments. So, it was fortunate that Akila was able to work with the Doctor on her last step forward into the unknown science of Magick. "Here you are, Doctor." Akila handed a thumb drive to Theoris.

Theoris took it and slide the black matte rectangular device into her computer's port. She clicked out several commands from the keyboard and hit the enter key. The Plasma flat-screen monitor pixilated a graph. Theoris' glasses slid to the tip of her nose. Subconsciously she pushed them back up. She nodded at the results and turned to Akila, who was waiting patiently. Theoris pressed her lips together. "This proves that anyone can perform magick."

Akila nearly shrilled with delight but squelched the impulse quickly. If Theoris could remain calm then she could to. She tried to sound as dry as Theoris sounded. "Yes, Doctor. Excellent news."

Theoris looked up at Akila and smiled. Her student was

13

working out perfectly. She was learning to control all irrational behavior and act and think objectively. Theoris considered herself blessed. Akila was brilliant, level headed, young, and cute all at the same time. Her poise and curvature was almost beguiling. Akila's two little ponytails rested on each shoulder. Theoris particularly liked and appreciated the sky blue bows at the end of each ponytail. She knew that Akila was going to make a lot of great contributions of her own one day. Theoris nodded. "Yes. The next thing we must do is begin experiments. The Human Trials Committee gave us the go ahead to start the studies again. We can experiment on one person. Do you have any suggestions, Akila?"

Akila smiled. "That is good news Doctor. I actually do have a suggestion." She had considered the Manifestation Theory correct. She had to. Why else spend all that time and money on getting this degree? "I was thinking that we need an individual who is already working in a position that would require an extreme belief in magick."

Theoris nodded and encouraged Akila to continue.

"We should be most careful of the extreme zealous cults. They tend to be over enthusiastic and might be a trifle dangerous."

"My thoughts exactly." Theoris said and pushed her glasses up.

"Maybe a local priest. Someone devoted to the trade, but not overly ambitious."

Theoris smiled. She nodded. "Excellent idea. I personally know the head priest of the Temple of Thoth, god of intellect, arts, writing, and all that is science. He's been trying to date me for the last ten years. Maybe I'll take him up on his tedious offer."

Both women giggled.

Honute rose early the next morning. He noticed Hypatia was not in bed. He heard clanking in the kitchen. He dressed himself in a slumber robe and walked out of the bedroom into the kitchen. Hypatia he noticed had discovered last night's dinner in the refrigerator. She had heated a leg and thigh of one of the game hens. The mushroom sauce was in a small pool next to the meat.

She dabbed a tear of monkey bread in the sauce, bit and chewed a piece off while eating a chunk of hen leg. She looked up and a frown formed on her face.

Honute chose to ignore the look and greeted her with a smile and a cheery, "Morning, Wife. How are you feeling?" He grabbed an empty cup and placed a bag of date and cilantro tea in the cup. Hypatia stared coldly at him. He felt her eyes pierce deep into the back of his neck as he filled his cup with water. He continued to ignore her as he side stepped to the microwave and placed the cup in and set the timer to sixty seconds. He took a deep breath, let it out, and turned to face Hypatia.

"I want a divorce." She said.

Honute froze in shocked surprise. "What?"

She repeated but this time the words came out biting. "I want a divorce."

Honute felt as if the words had teeth and ripped a piece of his heart away. He was at a loss as how to answer.

"Well, are you going to say anything?" Hypatia challenged.

"What would you have me say? 'Don't divorce me?'"

She answered, her upper lip curled in a way that made her look ugly. "Don't you want to know why?"

He nodded slowly. When she had that look on her face Pharaoh himself withdrew and hide.

"I no longer love you."

The microwave dinged.

Honute's head snapped back as if it were struck. "But why?" He started, "I know we don't see much of each other any more." He was at a loss and desperate for a way out. "We can make time. I'll ask Setenaju to ease my responsibilities. We can make it work. . ."

She cut him off and simply said. "You are not the man I thought I married."

"W-What do you mean?" He stammered out.

"You are weak and complacent." She said. "You have no ambition. All you do is tend to the Temple and sweep and wash at the feet of Thoth. You grab what is given to you instead of taking what you want."

"But, Hyp, you knew I wanted to be a Priest when you married me." He grabbed a chair next to her and sat down. He reached out to her hand.

She withdrew it as if his touch was venomous. She placed both hands in her lap.

Honute cleared his throat. "I told you from the beginning of our relationship that all I ever wanted to be was a priest. Nothing more."

She looked down at her hands, rage barely in check, and said with a clenched jaw, "I know, but I thought you were just being humble and didn't want to scare me away with boastful talk."

His face twisted up from hurt and disbelief.

"I was wrong." She said, her face turning a deeper pink. "I want someone ambitious, not a lower minion priest caring for an abject sycophantic god!"

Honute looked heavenward and uttered with conviction in his voice, "Oh, Lord-God Thoth, please forgive the words coming from Hypatia. Her heart is filled with hate, but it is not toward you. Please over look her. . ."

"Shut up!" She yelled. "I hate you and your god! You and your fawning over a god of letters!"

Honute slammed his hand on the table surprising both of them. "Thoth is not a lower god. He is part of the Ennead and must be given proper respect. As a scholar, Thoth should be your god. . ."

Hypatia got up from the table. "I no longer want to be with someone who is just content with bathing a statue. I'll be staying at the University. I told the landlord that you will be responsible for next month's rent. When you get back from your daily minion feet washing and blessing I'll be gone." She walked away into the bedroom and slammed the door.

Honute sat at the table in disbelief. What had he done wrong? Apparently, Isis hadn't heard his prays last night. He got up and walked to the bedroom. He lightly tapped on the door. "I need to dress and get ready for work." He tapped again.

A moment later the door opened up and Hypatia throw out some of his robes and sandals. She shut the door again, hard.

Honute gathered up his clothes in his arm as if they were a symbol of his pride. With a bowed head he walked into his office and got dressed. Luckily, he had access to the second bathroom that was between both rooms. Twenty minutes later he walked out of the apartment and followed the long worn path to the Temple of Thoth, god of intellect, arts, writing, and all that is science. Today he had to cleanse his thoughts and be pure of heart and mind. Today, Guriamon, the head priest wanted to talk to him. Honute prayed to Ma'at, Thoth's wife, for a good outcome. He needed it. The other shoe hadn't fallen yet.

Chapter 3

Ferruk entered his chamber. He slammed the door behind him, stormed over to his highboy and knocked all the contents off. Someone knocked at the door.

The door slowly opened and a capped head poked through. It was Arrutyi, his man servant. "Master, are you okay?"

Ferruk spun around and yelled. "Yes, I'm all right you fool!"

"It was that I heard. . ."

"Get out!"

Arrutyi backed his head out and started to slowly close the door.

"Wait!" Ferruk said. A smile formed on his face. He wouldn't have to perform any rituals until later this evening. He had time to enjoy the day and all the luxuries that came with power.

"Yes, Master?" He said stepping into the room.

"Draw my bath and have Ayruyi join me."

Arrutyi bowed out and closed the door. He hurried to tell his daughter that the Master had summoned her to attend him. It pained him that his daughter should also serve as Master's slave. But he and his daughter came from a long lineage of slaves. All the way back to Tutmoses III. They have always served the likes of the Royal family that was until recently. Pharaoh Futloramon IV gave his family servitude to Ferruk-amon Islat Huytrep-Ra, Mighty Priest of the Middle Lands. Ayruyi was but ten at the time. Her mother had passed away just a month before. It was a tragedy, but Pharaoh had favored Trequyi and he gave her a wonderful funeral. After that, things changed between his family and the Royal family. The Pharaoh no longer used him for special projects. Pharaoh even stopped placing a Poki flower on Trequyi grave. A month later the

Pharaoh gave Arrutyi and Ayruyi away to his present master. A most devious and evil vile creature. Arrutyi wondered why the gods would allow such a man to bless their lands and people. It was truly a mystery.

Ferruk stepped into the warm water. He grabbed a glass of wine offered to him and sipped at the content inside. He bent forward to expose his back. Ayruyi rubbed a sponge against it and let the soapy water cascade back into the tube. "Wash my front." He said and laid back. He parted his legs to let Ayruyi run the sponge between his legs. He smiled and sipped more of the wine. "You know Ayruyi, you have always been my favorite. Even Seth became envious when Futloramon gave me you."

Ayruyi continued to rub up and down. She replaced the sponge with her hand and massaged him. "Yes, Master."

Ferruk arched his back a little. "Take it and finish me off."

Ayruyi bent down and engulfed him with her mouth. She expertly stroked him. She would continue until she felt him swell and at the last second remove her lips and let him spend himself. She did this every day for as long as she could remember, and everyday she hated it. She sworn to the Goddess Isis that one day she would take his life and then to pay for her crime take her own life.

Ferruk moaned and tensed up. His body quivered as he spent himself in the bath water. After several seconds he grabbed Ayruyi hand and made her stroke him until he was hard again. When he was ready he told her to take off her clothes slowly. She obeyed and stepped into the tub. She straddled him and moved her body up and down tightening and loosening her legs in the process. Water splashed on the floor with each down stroke. Ferruk moaned deeply and nuzzled his face in Ayruyi's breast. He grabbed the sides of her hip and moved her up and down at his pace. Within seconds both cried out and collapsed. The water had turned cool and Ferruk shivered. "Get me a towel. I'm ready to get out."

Ayruyi forced herself to get up. She had become weak from her orgasm and she fought to move in a manner respectable of a slave doing her master's request. She dripped out of the tub, walked across the floor and grabbed a large fluffy towel from the rack. A dozen other towels sat puffed up and waiting. With the towel outstretched she waited for Ferruk to stand up. When he did she covered him and rubbed him dry. He walked over to a make-up desk and peered into the mirror. Ayruyi had his make-up case open. He took out his favorite eyeliner and began putting together his face. Ayruyi waited patiently, handing him various things he requested, shivering every now and then from a draft that breezed through the room.

Ferruk gave himself a smile in the mirror. He thought he looked handsome as usual and any woman who resisted his charm was a fool. He got up leaving Ayruyi wet and naked alone in the bathroom.

Ayruyi waited a few minutes before she allowed herself to shake uncontrollably. She drained the tub and scrubbed the sides and bottom harshly. Once she was satisfied that Ferruk's essence had been sucked down the drain did she draw a quick bath for herself. She made the water steaming hot and forced herself to accept the heat as a means to rid herself of his touch. She scrubbed hard. Ayruyi hated him and prayed to Isis that one day she would have the strength to erase him from the Blessed Lands. If not today, then maybe tomorrow. She scrubbed harder and nearly chafed her skin raw.

Chapter 4

Honute sat in the reception area waiting for Guriamon, High Priest of the Temple of Thoth. Honute had lead the early ritual of the Sun God Ra and the morning rites of Thoth. The prayers had been perfect. He hoped that Guriamon would appreciate his dedication and that punishment would not be too severe, though he couldn't remember if he had done anything wrong. Minutes passed quickly, at first. Then they passed slowly. Ten into fifteen, fifteen into twenty, thirty then forty. Honute waited.

Guriamon opened the door. "Ah, Honute, thank you for waiting so patiently. Come in."

Honute gathered himself and walked in. Two women were seated in front of Guriamon's desk. One looked to be in her late fifties and the other in her early twenties. Both were beautiful. The older one was dressed in a gray business skirt suit, a most un-Egyptian like attire. The younger one was more appropriately dressed in a traditional white cotton wrap. The edges were trimmed in dark blue and seemed to match her eyes. The wrap clung to her body in all the right places and Honute blushed by the decadent thought of his hands touching all those spots.

Akila watched as Honute walked in and stopped cold. He eyed Theoris first. She noted the quick display of emotion on his face. He disapproved of her business skirt, blouse and suit jacket. Theoris had told her that years ago she made a conscious effort to not wear traditional clothing. The Doctor felt that it demeaned women. Akila then locked eyes with the priest. He blushed and looked away.

Guriamon cleared his throat. "Honute, this is Dr. Theoris, Magick Manifestation Expert and her assistant Akila."

Honute nodded to each woman.

"You will be working with them. I'm releasing you from your duties . . ."

Honute's eyes popped open and his head snapped back as if he had been struck, hard. "But High Priest, have I done something wrong?"

Guriamon said, "No, no, nothing wrong. Quite the opposite actually."

Honute breathed a sigh of relief.

Guriamon continued, "You will help Dr. Theoris with her theory. You will continue to receive you regular pay and the Doctor is going to give you a sort of Per Diem for participating."

"Extra pay?" Honute said slowly.

Theoris stood up and said, "Priest Honute, your participation would be most important to my research." She stuck out her hand.

Honute looked down at it. His mind spinning and going in different places all at once. He saw his hand reach out and shake Dr. Theoris' hand but he didn't remember feeling her hand around his. He was in a daze and just let what happened happen. He remembered somewhere between shaking Theoris' hand and walking outside that he asked what her research was all about. She nearly sang out that it involved learning how to do magick. He laughed but stifled it when she gave him a stern look that suggested next time he was to ask for permission and the privilege to laugh out loud.

Ten minutes later Honute was sitting in the back seat of Dr. Theoris' car. She drove an expensive large luxury model that probably cost his entire years salary. He looked out the window as the car sped passed the various street merchants, playing children, and gutter urchins. New Heliopolis was built on the new plan of Enlightenment. Pharaoh himself oversaw the building of this city. Rumor had it that he built it on the words from the Oracle. She told Pharaoh that this new city would bring a fantastic and wonderful age to the Blessed Lands. That was what the rumors said. Maybe it was true, maybe not, but from the normal business in the streets it would take a miracle to bring about this new age.

Ferruk and the Oracle sat in her gathering chamber. Both sat at her large oval oak table with Ferruk sitting on her right side. She had her bowl out and colors started to swirl in a complex movement. She looked into it and started to moan and chant.

"Homage to you, Great God, the Lord of the double Ma'at! I have come to you, my Lord, I have brought myself here to behold your beauties. I know you, and I know your name, and I know the names of the two and forty gods, who live with you in the Hall of the Two Truths, who imprison the sinners, and feed upon their blood, on the day when the lives of men are judged in the presence of Osiris. In truth, you are 'The Twin Sisters with Two Eyes,' and 'The Daughters of the Two Truths.' In truth, I now come to you, and I have brought Ma'at to you, and I have destroyed wickedness for you. I have committed no evil upon men. I have not oppressed the members of my family. I have not wrought evil in the place of right and truth. . ."

Ferruk sat impatiently as the Oracle recited the mid chapter of The Coming in the Day from the Book of the Dead. She did this as a way of protection. Ferruk saw it as theatrics.

". . . I have not killed. I have not given the order to kill. I have not inflicted pain on anyone. I have not stolen the drink left for the gods in the temples. I have not stolen the cakes left for the gods in the temples. I have not stolen the cakes left for the dead in the temples. I have not fornicated. I have not polluted myself. I have not diminished the bushel when I've sold it. . "

Ferruk tried to stifle a loud yawn, he only half succeeded.

The Oracle continued ". . . I am pure. I am pure. I am pure. My purity is the purity the great heron in Heracleopolis. Behold, I am the nose of the God of Breath, who gives life to the people, on the day of completing the Eye of Ra in Heliopolis, on the last day of the second month of winter, In the presence of the pharaoh of this land. I have seen the Eye of Horus when it was full in Heliopolis!

Therefore, let no evil befall me in this land in this Hall of the Two Truths, because I know the names of all the gods within it, and all the followers of the great God."

Ferruk nearly fell asleep in the Oracle's half sphere, but caught himself in a snap jerk moment. If this hadn't been serious he would have laughed at himself.

The Oracle moaned loudly and said, "Behold."

The bowl of colors smoked and the contents swirled. An image appeared. A priest standing next to a young woman blurred from her side and reappeared. The scene changed and the priest rose high in the air, arms out stretched and legs crossed at the ankles. The priest spoke words but the bowl of future remained silent. Then the priest was dressed in all gold and he climbed the stairs of the Great Temple of Ra and sat in the High Priest Chair of Power – Ferruk's chair! The image disappeared

Ferruk's face was drained to pale white. He witnessed his end. "Can this be undone?" He asked the Oracle.

With her intense dark eyes she said, "Maybe."

"Maybe. How? You must tell me."

The Oracle got up and walked to an open doorway. "Come back tomorrow and I will have an answer for you."

Ferruk was furious for having been dismissed like this a second time. He fumed over the Oracle's seemingly lack of respect for his position. If Pharaoh hadn't favored this old crone to near worship he would have executed her on the spot. He stood up and chanced a glimpse in the bowl. He looked closely and thought he saw a word. The surface of the liquid shimmered and lapped at the edge of the bowl. A smile formed from his thin lips and he laughed as he stepped away from the table and walked out the Oracle's room of Gathering. The bowl had given him a clue. It gave him a name he occasionally looked up. It displayed, "THEORIS."

Chapter 5

The University of New Heliopolis was a gathering of large modern buildings. It covered an entire city block and was not unlike a small city within a large city. Theoris' car passed through the main gate. Honute stared out the window and swallowed hard.

Akila thought she heard something. She looked back and saw Honute gazing out the window. His face was nearly pressed firmly against the glass. "Is there something wrong, Priest Honute?"

Honute started breathing again. "Nothings wrong. It's just been awhile since I last visited here." He lied about nothing being wrong. Hypatia's office was buried somewhere within this small kingdom. The car traveled deeper and further into the little kingdom of science and mystery. Honute prayed to the one god that all this mighty institution claimed allegiance – Thoth, god of scribes, mathematicians, scientist, and everything erudite.

Hypatia walked into her office and over to a small counter against the wall. On it was a small refrigerator, coffee maker and a microwave. She poured herself a cup of steaming coffee and sat at her desk. The window behind her had a view of nearly the entire campus. She could see the entrance way and the main parking lot. She had a lot of stories about the goings on in the parking lot after hours. She turned her chair around and faced the window. She thought of the meeting she had only minutes ago. The Chairman of the Board and CEO of the University gave her news. The University was promoting her officially to Head Lecturer and Chair of Astronomy. Also, the school was temporarily relieving her of her secondary duties and several other lesser lecturers would be assigned to her as assistants – that was, until the school hired her permanent staff. When her predecessor left he took his entire staff. This left her to perform his, hers, and all the in between duties. It had been exhausting. Everyday she would drag herself home to find Honute relaxing in his office reading over his prayer book. He always had dinner ready and he joyfully did all the household chores. Hypatia needed only ask and Honute would do it. Being a dutiful husband was the least of her worries. He did it all and without complaining. Even his love making was dutiful. He never failed in quenching her sometimes seemingly insatiable sexual appetite. Honute some how knew when, where, and what to do. Bringing on one wave after another wave of blissful intense orgasms. Then when he was certain her hungry had been satiated would he allow himself a minuscule amount of pleasure. Even after love making he was respondent to her needs. Sleeping on the wet side of the bed or fetching clean sheets. He often loved lighting candles and burning wonderfully smelling incense. Hypatia loved cedar wood and recently Glycerin Aloe. It was just recently that she realized she wasn't really happy. Honute was what many woman dream of marrying. A caring sensitive attentive dutiful husband who worshiped the very ground you walked on. What she came to believe she wanted was a go-getter. She wanted Honute to be at the top of his game instead of sitting on the sidelines passing out bottles of water. She wanted him to tell her that he had a rough day firing half a dozen people and that the old man pissed him off so bad he had to tell him where to stick it. And then he would tell her how impressed the old man was by his ass chewing that he would give him a raise. That's what she wanted to hear. Not some meaningless dribble about how he blessed a hundred pilgrims in two hours or that the head priest was inspired by his morning Sun ritual. She wanted Honute to be reckless, daring, adventurous, aggressive. She wanted him to be like the men in those romance novels. Men who had a hard edge about them that screamed 'I could cut your throat just as I look at you!' She wanted Honute to be bad. Hypatia had been daydreaming for nearly an hour while looking out the window. Dr. Theoris' car pulled into her parking spot. It was right next to hers. She read the Doctor's memo on her proceeding to the next step in her research. The University had been all abuzz about her new theory on Magick. Everyone believed in it, but not everyone was capable of doing it. That is until now. The Doctor had requested some of the University's resources – medical, physics, electronics, anything and everything to measure, record, and hopefully reproduce results. Even her department would be involved. And as head of the Astronomy department she was in control of the Zettatron, the most powerful and sensitive cyclotron in the southern half of the Blessed Lands.

Theoris parked the car in her assigned spot. Honute watched with a growing sickening feeling as Hypatia's car came into sight. Of all the worst luck in the Blessed Lands would this happen to him. His wife's car inches away from his face. Dread covered him in a cold and icy touch – the gods have not been good to him.

Akila noticed the pale face of Honute. "Priest Honute? Are you sure you are all right?"

Honute swallowed hard and shook his head. "That is my wife's car."

Theoris placed the car in park. She looked over her shoulder at Honute. "You're Dr. Hypatia's husband?" She looked closer. "Ah, yes. The last Joyous celebration. I remember. Funny how one forgets certain details."

Honute didn't remember Theoris but he remembered the celebration. One of the other residential professors, Dr. Turtukilo, had embarrassed himself. Apparently, he had gotten drunk, with three other faculty members, and was caught head bobbing on one of them. Honute himself had stumbled on the orgy. He had been looking for the restroom. He backed away giving his most sincere apologies and stepped into the Chairman of the Board. He, too, had been looking for the restroom.

Akila said with a little bit of sadness in her voice, "But why would that be a problem?"

He took a deep breath. "This morning she asked me for a divorce."

Akila said, "Oh. Sorry to hear that."

"She said she would be staying at the University."

Theoris thought about that. "I don't think it'll be too much of a problem. We really don't have to go anywhere near the Astronomy department. We may not even need to use the Zettatron's magnetometers. We could probably requisite one of the portable models."

Honute nodded.

Theoris said, "Of course, the occasional running into each in the hallway may not be entirely avoided. Is this going to be a problem?"

Honute shook his head. "I don't think so. She was pretty calm about it. It should be very civil . . . and awkward."

Theoris nodded, opened the car door and got out. The others followed.

Hypatia noted that two other individuals were in Dr. Theoris' car. Theoris got out first, followed by a younger woman, Akila was her name, if memory served Hypatia correctly. She took a mouth full of coffee as the third person stepped out the car. It was Honute! Coffee splattered on the window. She grabbed several tissues from the box on her desk and wiped the window clean. She saw Theoris, the younger woman and her husband walk into the Psychology, Cognition, and Behavior building across the street. 'Oh boy' was her thought. 'When things got better did they get worse?'

Chapter 6

Honute followed Dr. Theoris and Akila through the double doors leading into the building. They only had to walk past a few doors to reach Theoris' main office. Honute stepped in and saw all sorts of electronic equipment. Monitors against the wall, long thin neon bulb like fixtures and lots of wires on the floor.

"Mind the wires." Theoris said stepping over a branch of twisty vine like strands. "We'll set up in the smaller office. Akila, could you take Priest Honute there. I'm going to gather a few things. I'll be back in a bit. Make him feel at home, please."

Akila nodded. "Please follow me, Priest Honute." Honute followed Akila into a small office. A couch ran along one wall, a desk and two chairs against the other. On the third wall was a table that had a small refrigerator, a cardboard box with stuff in it, a microwave, and a coffee maker. This office had a window view. He noted Theoris' vanity wall. She had all her awards, certificates, commendations, and all sorts of other recognition nailed and pasted up. Honute walked over to the wall and noted several Ph.D plaques. A commendation plaque was next to them. 'In recognition for service above the call of duty the collective regions of the Blessed Lands awards Dr. Theoris this plaque of Commendation.' It was dated about ten years ago. Around the same time Honute served in the War against the Infidels. He noted that Theoris received the Commendation for identifying and later coming up with a cure for the Night Sweat plague. A bio-weapon developed by the Infidels. Honute, himself, escaped several strikes. He moved on to the next item – this particular plaque drudged up nightmares he wished to not live again. The War was the reason why he became a priest. He had enough killing and murdering humans in the name of defense and the preservation of the Blessed Lands. Luckily, Pharaoh and the Cursed Lands, as his fellow compatriots loved to call it, agreed on a truce. It had been six years now. A little more than the length of his marriage. Honute hoped that his pending marriage disaster would not be the coming sign of war.

Akila watched Honute move from plaque to plaque. She found him strangely curious. His physical build seemed that of a soldier, but he behaved like a humbled soul. She noted the slim waist and solid arms and thighs under his plain cotton robe. It wasn't tight on him and it wasn't too big either. It just seemed to fit him so well. He moved gracefully, like he had been a dancer or performed in one of the traveling circuses. And his eyes spoke volumes about the man. Not once had she seen them unfocused. He seemed to note everything within his view. She remembered how he stared out the window and took anything in. The cars, the people, the buildings, everything. To her, Honute seemed to be an enigma. "Priest Honute, may I get you anything while we wait for Dr. Theoris?"

"Call me Honute." He said while staring at another 'I love me' plaque.

Akila caught herself smiling. She wiped it off her face. "Okay, Honute. May I get you anything? Water, tea?" She left it at that.

"Tea sounds nice." He turned around and caught her staring at him. He smoothly smiled back. "Are you having tea as well?"

She hadn't planned on it, but it made sense to drink with Honute. "We don't have a lot of flavors. Raspberry, Lemon Date, Kiwi Aloe, and Bark."

Honute said, "I'll take the Bark."

Akila walked over to the table with the coffee maker. She reached into the cardboard box of stuff and pulled out a box of tea. She then reached into the refrigerator and pulled out a plastic one gallon container of water. She poured a third of the water into the coffee maker and placed a half dozen bags of tea in the plastic pullout top. After replacing the container of water and the box of tea she turned the coffee maker on. She heard the drip hiss sizzle of the water as it gurgled its way from the tubing inside the coffee maker. After several seconds a dark brown liquid poured into the clear coffee pot. Akila reached into the box again and grabbed two yellow plastic cups.

Another minute later Honute and Akila were sitting on the couch sipping Bark tea. Honute particularly liked Bark because of its bitter aftertaste bite. It had a sort of thin oily texture when it touched the tongue but went watery after a second or two inside the mouth. Then the aftertaste was so bitter that it tasted almost sweet. And Akila made it strong – the way he liked it.

"Am I really going to learn magick, Akila?"

Akila had been quietly sipping her tea. Dr. Theoris had been gone for nearly fifteen minutes. Akila didn't want to stare at Honute, but she wanted to study his face. His skin was a little dry but that was due, she reasoned, to the arid air most of the time during the summer months. She noted his eyebrows. Not thick but not thin. She didn't think he would look good with the current fad of men plucking their eyebrows until both were paper thin. She decidedly thought he looked much better natural. "Yes, we at least hope so. Dr. Theoris identified the gene responsible for controlling our ability to do magick. She thinks that we all have the capability. It's just only a matter of learning how to trigger the gene."

Honute took a sip of tea and let the liquid linger on his tongue. He felt the warm liquid slide down his throat and heat up his insides. "Really?" He was intrigued, but the nagging thought that Hypatia was probably one or maybe two buildings away kept him from completely relaxing and enjoy Akila's company. "But why me? I'm just a simple priest."

"Being a simple priest is exactly why she chose you. In order for us to be successful we need someone who is religiously dedicated but not overly zealous."

Honute laughed. "Over zealous you'll find I'm not."

Akila smiled and Honute found himself smiling back. It was her lips he was most drawn to. When she relaxed her face her lips had a natural part to them. The top and bottom would separate just enough to show a little bit of teeth. He also liked the way she blushed.

"The person must also have good focusing ability."

Honute nodded. "But how will you know?"

"The first thing would be to get a baseline record."

"Baseline?"

Akila nodded, "Yes, record your brain and physiological activity. Record your DNA and identify other useful markers, run test on your meditative ability, and test how deeply and easily you can go into a trance."

Honute sipped the tea. "A lot of stuff. Then I'll learn how to do magick?"

Akila smiled, "We hope so. I hope you are not averse to receiving medication?"

"Medication?" Honute almost choked on his tea. "What type of medication exactly?"

Akila regretted she mentioned the drugs. Dr. Theoris wanted to get Honute comfortable with them before she would tell him about the drugs. But the conversation had been going so nicely. She swallowed hard and slowly answered, "I will be honest with you. We are going to do a lot of things. Some are going to be pleasant while others are going to be a bit uncomfortable. Everything will be completely safe and there is no risk to you well being. . ."

"But what type of medication?" Honute pressed.

Akila took a deep breath. "Some will be psychotropic and others would have physiological effects on you."

Honute tried to keep a distressed look from his face and his voice. "Such as?"

"Such as controlling your blood pressure and heart rate."

"Oh." Was all he said. Honute took a big sip from the cup. The tea had gotten cold and tasted bad. "I think we need to heat up the tea."

Akila nodded and automatically collected the cups, walked over to the microwave, and placed them in the center. She set the timer to thirty seconds. "Honute, it will be safe, for the most part. There is a chance that something could go wrong, but Dr. Theoris is very skilled and she will have a staff of medical personnel working with her."

Honute became unfocused and drifted back to a time when he was cold wet and miserable. It was about seven years ago and the war was not going well. He led his squad over a hill and right smack in the middle of the enemy. It was about twenty of them. IQ said the area was clear for at least another ten aturs. Hell broke loose when they cleared a clump of trees. The enemy hyped up on STIM took them by surprise. Half the squad had been killed in less than a second. Honute had been wounded before he stepped behind a large tree for cover. He surveyed the area and spotted the enemy about half a 'minute of march' away. Pieta, Kiluyt, Figuli, and Saviofa were firing back. Honute figured he could toss a grenade the full distance if he had the proper coverage. He yelled out that he needed cover soon. He pulled the pin loose and yelled 'grenade!' The entire area was sprayed with automatic fire. A second later the grenade concussioned the enemy. Honute threw five more to make sure he got them all. When it was silent he limped over and poked at several of the bodies. All dead. He checked the pocket of one and pulled out a hypo spray syringe. It hadn't been used yet. On the outside cover it had writing in the Infidel's language STIM. The enemy had doped up and attacked them.

Honute refocused his eyes. "I'm sorry I drifted."

Akila looked him in the eyes. "Where'd you go?" She handed him a warm cup of tea.

"A rather bad place. I served in the war." He lowered his head.

"Oh." Akila said and she sipped at her tea. After several seconds of silence she asked, "Was it bad?"

Honute nodded. "The enemy had been hyped up on drugs . . ." He trailed off.

Akila thought for a moment. Her eyes opened wide in comprehension. "Ah, I see." She sipped at the tea again. She was excited because she understood what he meant. He didn't have to completely spell it out for her. "Will this be a problem?"

He looked her straight in the eyes. He wanted to say 'What do you think?' but instead said, "I don't believe so. I just have this thing about drugs and medication. Pharaoh's Royal Army would sometimes have us use drugs to fight better. After the truce I got out and became a priest."

Akila nodded in understanding. Her father had served in Pharaoh's Royal Army and had been killed in action. It was the worst time of her life. Her father being killed and later her mother getting cancer, but she was a big girl now and she knew her parents would be proud of her – if only they were alive. She smiled sweetly and innocently at Honute. She really wanted to get to know him better. A soldier and then a priest. It must have been really horrible she thought. "You need not worry. It will be safe and you would be doing a service to the Blessed Lands."

Honute sipped again and smiled. Yes, he really did like Akila. She had a smile that would smooth away all the troubles in the world. He secretly wondered if she was seeing someone or dating, but then he banished those thoughts. He was probably her father's age. Besides, she was way to smart for a humble man as himself. She seemed full of life and energy, almost like Hypatia. Then it hit him. She seemed to be very much like Hyp. Her mannerisms, the way she walked into a room, how she sat, and her smile. She smiled not just with her lips but with her entire face. She probably had Hypatia's drive and ambition he thought. Hypatia was probably right to leave him. He was too complacent for the likes of an ambition woman. He sighed and gave Akila a smile. "Tell me more about this program. How are we to make magick?"

Dr. Theoris walked into Hypatia's office. Hypatia had been staring out the window when she noticed Theoris purposefully walk out the building, across the parking lot, and into her building. She figured the good Doctor wanted to discuss some points, so it didn't surprise her when Theoris walked through the office threshold.

"May we talk?" Theoris asked.

Hypatia turned her chair around, leaned back and said, "Why of course. Anything in particular you'd like to discuss?"

Theoris stepped up to the desk. "Yes actually. I'll cut to the chase."

Hypatia nodded.

"Your husband is here."

"I know. I saw him walk into the building with you."

Theoris eased up a bit. She stood a little more relaxed and not as aggressive. "He is my research subject."

Hypatia nodded again and sat with her back straight against her chair. She absolutely dreaded this. "I understand."

Theoris stared down at the other woman. "I know about the pending divorce."

Hypatia swallowed hard. She nodded.

"And I'm hoping that the marital issue between the two of you will not interfere with this research."

Hypatia couldn't do anything but listen to Dr. Theoris. For years Theoris had been the dominating force behind the University. Even the Chairman of the Board and CEO bowed down to her influence. Disagreeing with her would be so much as career suicide. She lifted her chin up. "Honute and I are able to work this out amiable. It shouldn't be a problem. I told him that I will be staying here at the University until I found a place of my own."

Theoris nodded approvingly and smiled. Her face lightened up and she seemed to have relaxed a bit more.

Hypatia wondered what other bit of personal information Honute told her. It pissed her off that Theoris was in her office throwing her weight around. This was her office and she didn't appreciate the bitch doing this. 'Screw you,' was her thought but she instead said, "Dr. Theoris, you know you will have my full cooperation in your research. You have nothing to worry about."

Theoris' face brightened. "That's what I figured. I just had to be sure."

Hypatia thought 'self-righteous bull bitch.'

Theoris pulled up a chair and sat. "I hope I'm not disturbing you or anything. I'd like to discuss with you a possible joint paper on some of my research."

'The bitch just made herself at home!' "Not at all. A joint paper sounds wonderful. What in particular would I be able to make a contribution?"

Theoris rested her shoulders against the chair. Her lower back was away from the chair and the effect made her look like she was slouching.

Hypatia tried not to stare but it was at best difficult not to notice the older woman sitting with such bad posture. She tried to maintain eye contact with Theoris and noticed the Doctor looking intently at her.

Theoris rested in the chair and allowed herself to relax. She eyed Hypatia in a way that would make most individuals uncomfortable. She noted how Hypatia's chest rose and fell with her breathing and how supple her breasts were. Theoris wished that Hypatia was not sitting behind her desk. She wanted to see all of her. From her shoulder length hair to the tight clinging cotton wrap she worn to the tips of her pretty painted toes. Hypatia was definitely someone Theoris wanted to get to know. She thought how interesting it was that she noticed her much more knowing that she was divorcing Honute. Maybe it was the thought that she was no longer attached to a man and that she would find herself alone at night. Very late at night. "Oh, I almost forgot. Congratulations on your recent appointment."

Hypatia replied, "Thank you. I didn't think it would happen soon enough."

Theoris nodded. "Well, when the Chairman asked me about filling the position I couldn't think of a better person then the one working in the position. You know how some men are, not particularly imaginative."

Hypatia held in her shock and surprise. Theoris implicitly admitted that she had some part in her finally getting this position.

"It is obvious that women are the more superior." And she laughed.

Hypatia laughed with her and worried why the Doctor was becoming so chummy. Last week, she barely got a nod of recognition. Now Theoris was chatting as if they were good friends.

Theoris sat slowly straight in the chair. She cleared her throat. "Do you have any plans to celebrate your promotion?"

Hypatia swallowed hard. "I hadn't thought about it. I hadn't expected the promotion. If I were to go home Honute would insist on cooking a celebration meal, blessings and everything. But all this morning my thoughts were only of getting a cot placed in this office. . ."

"A cot!" Theoris blurted out.

Hypatia nodded and pressed her lip inward and together.

"Why not a hotel? Any relatives in New Heliopolis?"

Hypatia shook her head. "I have family over in the Four Corners area. And I was trying to save a little money."

Theoris chortled. "You got a promotion. You should be thinking big now. Don't tell me Honute controls all the accounts and credit cards?"

"No, I handle all that. I didn't want to take all the money. His salary would never pay for the rent, I did that, but I didn't want to leave him without a place to live. At least not for another month or two."

"How sweet of you Hypatia! I can see some of the reason why he married you. Very thoughtful. Okay, tonight you will be my guest."

Hypatia was horrified. "Thank you, Doctor Theoris, but I couldn't impose."

"Call me, Theoris. We are equals now, and you would not be imposing. I have a house that is way too large and empty for me. It'll be nice to have some company and it'll be much more comfortable that some old cot."

"But, Doc . . . Theoris that is so generous of you."

"Nope, not another protest. I insist. You will be my guest tonight and I am going to take you out to celebrate." And she gave Hypatia a steely cold gaze.

Hypatia felt a cold chill envelope her body. She felt trapped and tricked. Her mind raced to find a graceful way out of being Theoris' guest. But she couldn't come up with something satisfactory. She felt powerless and couldn't see a 'safe' way out of this predicament. "Yes, Theoris." Then she thought, 'I'm gonna make you pay for my company. Expensive dinner, expensive drinks, expensive deserts. Wait and see! I'll cost you so much money tonight it'll be cheaper for you to pay for my hotel room for a month.' And she relaxed and smiled. The evening won't be so bad after all. Honute can eat his meal over his prayer book. She would dine on caviar, water crest crackers, lobster, two hundred deben wine, and super rich, high fat, high cholesterol desert.

Chapter 7

"I will kill him, Father." Ayruyi stabbed the air with a short sword. "I will kill him and we will be free."

Arrutyi grabbed at the sword. He gently took it out of his daughter's hands. "Ayruyi, you mustn't talk like this. High Priest Ferruk is our master. That is the way of things."

"No father. It can't be. What kind of Blessed Lands is this if we have to be owned by vile creatures such as him?" She reached for the sword.

"Daughter, that's the way it has always been. Pharaoh saw fit to give us to our master. We have to be thankful that he keeps us in comfort." He kept the sword away.

"Father, give me the sword. When he sleeps tonight I can run it through his heart before he knows what happened."

"And you would be publicly executed."

Ayruyi said nothing.

"I don't want to lose my only daughter. You are all I have left worth living for in this world."

Ayruyi looked down at the ground and pouted. She was torn between murdering and not murdering Ferruk. Every time he touched her she wanted to rip her skin off. He poisoned her soul each time he caressed her. She lost her compassion and humanity a little at a time. "Father, I hate him."

Arrutyi reached an arm around Ayruyi's shoulders. "Ayruyi, you have to have patience. I can't explain it but one day we will be free. One day we will both be able to walk the streets of the Blessed Lands with our chin up. But we have to have trust in Osiris, Isis, and Ra."

Ayruyi turned and buried her face into his shoulders sobbing.

She felt utterly helpless and realized she hated her father as well. He accepted their fate and talked of patience. 'Damn him,' she thought but she found his arms around her soothing. 'The power of a father's love can be no less than the love from a god.' Ayruyi cried harder and hugged her father back.

Ferruk sat at his computer and called up the records of Dr. Theoris. It wasn't rocket science for him to figure out that the Oracle's bowl gave him the name of a person. It was unexpected that he would know the person. He wondered if it was divine providence that made the Oracle tire and walk away from the bowl. No doubt if the Oracle saw the name she would have given him some near forgotten tome and called it her own. She would have put a twisted and mangled spin so bad that he would have been up late for weeks trying to figure out what she really meant. And by the time he did figure it out it would have been too late. He secretly thought that she purposely did this to keep him off balanced or ill-prepared. Ferruk took the thought of having the Oracle standing in front of a bullet-riddled wall waiting for execution as a prediction. He daydreamed the same scenario many times and came to the conclusion that actually killing her would be the only way for him to get a good night sleep. Anything less than that would be his punishment.

Theoris walked into the office and sat down at her desk. Akila and Honute were chatting away. She thought 'good' because it would make things easier. Theoris decided to let Akila handle the first few initial stages of the research.

Akila got up from the couch. "May I get you anything Doctor?"

Theoris leaned back in the chair and smiled. "Akila, is that Bark tea?"

"Yes, ma'am. Would you like a cup? There's a quarter pot left. Or if you like I can fix you something different."

"Bark tea would be just fine." Theoris looked at Honute and she wondered what type of man he was. Minutes ago she hit on his wife now she was in the same room acting like nothing unusual or inappropriate happened. He seemed like a nice enough person.

Akila placed a yellow cup of Bark tea in front of Theoris. She walked back to the couch and sat next to Honute.

Theoris noted Akila sat with her body a little too stiff. She wondered if the younger woman was trying to conceal her feelings for Honute. She lifted the cup up to her mouth and inhaled deeply. The aroma from the tea gave her a tingly sensation. She sipped at the tea and let the liquid rest on her tongue. She savored the taste and swallowed after several seconds. The room had been pointedly quiet since she walked in on the two. "Well, Priest Honute . . ."

"Please call me Honute."

Theoris nodded. "Okay Honute. Do you have any questions?"

"Well, Akila was about to tell me how you planned on getting me to make magick." He sipped his tea.

"You want the five hour lecture or the one minute answer?"

Honute laughed. "It has been awhile since I've been in school. How about the one minute answer and then later you can give me that lecture. I find it fascinating and intriguing if not a little bit scary."

Theoris laughed herself. Despite Honute being a man she found herself warming up to him. She couldn't put her finger on it, but there was definitely something about him. Maybe it was his relaxed demeanor or that maybe he seemed to have learned a healthy dose of humility. Either way he seemed a dichotomy. Powerful build but compassionate career choice that required sensitivity and empathy. She sipped at the tea again. 'He is going to find out if I successfully seduce her.' She told herself. Guilt surfaced and she felt its sting. Not to the point of being intolerable, but enough to be a bother. She brushed the feeling aside. "My theory about Manifested Magick is that at some point in our past we humans were capable of influencing objects around us. I call it the 'survival trick.' Maybe it was a little telekinesis to shake and move bushes and trees to confuse predators. Or maybe even communicate between one another during hunting – on some level animals seem to have this ability. Or maybe we could heal our sick and injured by laying hands. The fact is I don't really know what type of magick you are going to do. The gene we've identified is possibly the trigger mechanism for some sort of process. What I think and hope will happen is that once we get this gene to trigger it'll start a chemical process in your body that will start a cascade of other chemical processes that will eventually allow you to manipulate objects."

Honute sipped his tea and listened attentively. "Manipulate objects? As in make them move?"

Theoris sipped her tea and nodded. "Yes, telekinesis. I identified very fine and small receptacles at the ends of our finger tips. It's amazing really. The receptacles seem to be vestigial. My thoughts are that given the proper chemical reaction small electrically charged particles would accumulate. And by means of quantum mechanics could influence distance molecules."

Honute's mind raced. Was Dr. Theoris a nut or did she really believe she could make him produce magick? He looked at Akila for a second and back to Theoris. Both stared back at him. He wasn't sure if he should just get up and walk out or take them seriously. He just didn't know. He drained the cup of the last of the Bark tea. Maybe she did have something, really. He had always believed in the gods and their ability to do magick. Maybe there was really a scientific reason. Just maybe she could pull this off. The question was, "What was he going to get out of this? Fortune? Fame? Power and money? All of which sounded assuredly unpleasant. He just wanted a simple and content filled life. A happy wife, a nice job, great kids, and a restful future – read retirement. "Will it be harmful?"

"To do magick?" Theoris drained her cup. "I don't know. I won't lie to you. We are going to have to do this in steps. And if it works you will be famous."

Honute's face paled. "Famous is not what I want!"

Akila placed her hand on top of his. "You'll be able to do magick, maybe even help people."

Theoris smiled. Akila was indeed an excellent assistant. "It really is your choice. I'll make you a promise. If it starts to get too rough and terrible you can walk away."

Honute looked into Akila's eyes and he almost melted. He looked back at Theoris and he considered her words. 'I could always back out if he wanted to,' was his thought. He looked back at Akila. She smiled sweetly and squeezed his hand reassuringly. "Okay." He said. He felt his fate sealed by that one word and he only hoped Thoth would protect him.

Ferruk read Dr. Theoris' biography. It read like some sort of made for AV fiction. Super genius was an understatement of a title. Even he was mentioned, though he was just a small foot note. Of course, that would change. He had his plans – he smiled and stared momentarily into empty air. He refocused, inhaled deeply and let it out. She even had Pharaoh's ear and also had the title, 'Royal friend.' He printed out her bio and placed the sheets in a folder. New Heliopolis was about five hundred miles south. Tomorrow he would make arrangements to meet with Dr. Theoris and see where she fitted into the Oracle's vision. She was the key to all this. He felt it. It had to be divine providence that all this was happening now.

Chapter 8

Honute ate dinner alone. Dr. Theoris took him home and sped off into the distance. She said she would pick him up bright and early tomorrow morning. She suggested that he get a good night sleep. They would have a very busy day of testing and basically getting a baseline on him. He was disappointed when he found out that Akila didn't own a car and therefore can't drop him off. He picked at his food as he thought about all that transpired in the last 24 hours. He was getting a divorce, he would learn how to do magick, and he met the most wonderful woman, Akila. Maybe Thoth had something special in store for him. He couldn't help but wonder the significance of Akila giving him a firm reassuring squeeze on the hand.

Hypatia sat across from Theoris. Both had just finished dinner and now waited for a servant to bring desert. Hypatia stuffed herself with delicious food and several glasses of wine. Her face was warm and there was a slight numbness at the tip of her nose. She giggled, brushed her hair out of her face, and drained her glass.

Theoris watched with amusement at how Hypatia unwound. She knew the woman had been under a lot of stress in the past several months and this displayed facetious jocularity was refreshing. She poured Hypatia another glass of honey wine and briefly touched her on the hand. Hypatia's skin was warm to the touch and just watching the young woman's giddiness was infectious. Theoris poured herself a glass of wine. "To a most brilliant and beautiful woman."

Hypatia almost choked on a mouthful of wine. She smiled, looked at Theoris, and blushed. It had been a long time since anyone had paid this much attention to her. She felt almost guilty that she was actually enjoying the attention. "And to a most brilliant and beautiful woman herself." She drained the glass.

Theoris smiled and leaned in closer. "You know Hypatia, I find you very attractive."

Hypatia grinned with pressed lips. "Thank you, Theoris, but I have to admit this makes me a little uneasy."

Theoris nodded. "Too soon?"

Hypatia nodded and looked down. "I just don't know where my emotions lie. I do love Honute, but I also don't love him at the same time."

Theoris filled both glasses.

"One morning I woke up and he seemed to not be the man I married. Oh, he's a wonderful husband, don't get me wrong. He's just not the wonderful I want." She looked up into Theoris' eyes. "Does that make sense?"

The older woman slowly nodded. "It does make sense. Many years ago I was married."

Hypatia said, "Really? I had no idea."

"Most people don't know. We had been married for about ten years. He was pretty successful. A priest for the Temple of Osiris Ani over in Thebes. He was twenty and I was sixteen when we married. We had a wonderful life. I doted over him and would have done anything to make him happy. He was equally loving and encouraged me to get an education. Later things changed?"

"What happened?"

"I realized that he wasn't married to me any longer. He was married to the temple and the priesthood. He was on the fast track to success and took advantage of ever opportunity that came his way. He started out as a priest like Honute, doing simple but important tasks, and as the years went by he took on more and more responsibility. Then one day he was promoted to Head Priest of the local town and that's when I realized he was not the man I married. He was a complete stranger."

Hypatia nodded in understanding.

"He was consumed by power and authority. Luckily, I had just received my Ph.D in Theoretical physics and was able to take a job as an assistant lecturer at the local college. The minute after I received my first paycheck I told him I wanted a divorce. He was furious and threw a fit. He threw anything that was within reach that didn't weigh more than a hundred pounds. I was terrified and ran out the house." She sipped at the wine. Her face flushed red and felt warm. She was tingly all over and welcomed the euphoric feeling. "I hadn't seen Ferruk in twenty years. Though I have followed his rise to power."

"What does he do now?" Hypatia asked. She got warm and seriously wanted to take off her wrap. She was certain Theoris wouldn't mind, but she had to consider the restaurant. The guest would be horrid if she sat naked and drinking.

"He's the Vizier and Head Priest of the Middle Lands."

Hypatia blinked. "Really? I thought I recognized the name. He was your husband?"

Theoris nodded.

"Wow. He is the person I wanted Honute to be."

Theoris sipped more of the wine. "Be lucky he's not. Trust me. Power does change a man. I saw him go from my beloved husband to an insensitive stranger. He may even had a few affairs." Theoris reached her hand out and lightly grasped Hypatia's. "Hypatia, as much as I hate saying this, Honute is a wonderful man. His heart is in the right place and you may not ever get a man sweeter than he. I ought to have my head examined for saying this. Here I am trying to seduce you and I'm compelled to tell you to consider carefully your reason for divorcing him."

Hypatia listened and lightly squeezed Theoris' hand back. "Thank you for being honest and sharing something very personal. I have thought about it. Honute is not the man for me. I don't know what I want really. Maybe I will change my mind, maybe I won't. I just know, right now, right here, he is not the one."

The servant finally brought the desert and left. A large quarter slice of chocolate cake. Layered into three levels. Chocolate, chocolate, and of course chocolate. The top and middle level icing was a cream rich blended swirl of chocolate and cocoa butter.

Hypatia looked up and smiled. "Can we take this back to your place. The wine must be getting to me. I'm a little warm."

Theoris snapped her fingers at a servant. "Check please."

Akila stayed up late. She lay on her bed starring at the ceiling. Her mind spun in a slow spiral thinking about Honute. Everything she knew told her that he was not the kind of man she wanted. Everything she felt told her otherwise. She sensed that he was kind and gentle, but he also had an unmistakable hard and sharp edge. Her choice of prospective dating material would be someone with an IQ well over one hundred eighty. He might wear eye glasses, or he might not. He would be good in some sports and have a wonderful sense of humor. Akila hadn't known Honute long enough to know if he had one. Did he tell priest jokes, or could he cut it with the big leaguers. She sighed and rolled onto her left side. Her digital clock displayed 2:00 am. She rolled to the right, got exasperated and got out of bed. She walked over to her computer and logged into the Blessed Land Knowledge Repository. She looked up Thoth and the Mighty Temple of Thoth. She also did a search on Priest Honute – just to see if he had anything on record. After ten minutes of searching she instructed the service to send an alert when and if there was a hit. She figured nothing would come of it, but one never knew the results of probing into someone's life. All sorts of nasty and deliciously scandalous tidbits could surface.

Chapter 9

Theoris pulled the car into the driveway. It was late and the two women staggered out of the car and to the front door. Theoris lived in a two story five bedroom house. From what Hypatia could see of the lawn, in the dark, was that Theoris loved colorful plants. The moon cast a subdued light over the area creating a surreal scene of shaded and dark colors. Leafy plants lined the walkway on either side toward the door. Several small trees dotted the lawn and one large tree hung menacingly over the house. Hypatia almost lost her footing. She looked up into the top half of the tree and didn't notice where she was going. She had to lean on Theoris to keep from tripping. During the drive the honey wine crept up on her and attacked. She was more than tipsy, she was drunk. Theoris struggled for her keys and dropped them twice. Both women giggled. She scooted her skirt up high and knelt down to retrieve the keys. She nearly fell into her well groomed hedge. The one immediately right of the door. After a moment she was able to slip the keys into the lock. The key turned smoothly and the door opened suddenly. Both women tumbled in. A lamp, somewhere, fell, crashed, and broke into many pieces. Theoris laughed and said, "Oops. I'll have to get a new one."

Hypatia slurred, "I'm slorry. Was it expesive?"

Theoris giggled. "No, it was a gift from the CEO. I hated it but couldn't come up with a good enough honest excuse to get rid of it."

Hypatia giggled in reply. "The honey wine snuck up on me. I seem to be drunk." She struggled to the living room and collapsed on a couch.

Theoris took the cake into the kitchen. After a few minutes

rummaging around she came out with two flute glasses and a bottle of wine. She grinned and sat next to Hypatia.

"Aren't we drunk enough?" Hypatia said and collapsed into the couch cushions.

"Here," Theoris said handing her a glass and pouring wine into it. "We have to finish this first. Besides, it's still early."

Hypatia looked at her watch. Through bloodshot eyes she read 10:00 pm. "Aren't you going to give me the dollar tour?" She said struggling to get to her feet. "Or point me to the bathroom."

Theoris drained the glass and said, "Follow me." She put the glass on the coffee table, grabbed Hypatia's hand and led her, in a zig zag sort of way, through the house. She stopped every now and then and pointed out the various rooms. "The main bathroom, the second bedroom, my main office, my workshop –"

"You have a workshop?"

"Yep. I build things as a hobby." And they staggered to the main bedroom. "My bedroom."

The room was very large and spacious. The wood floor was polished to a high sheen and a handful of thick threaded rugs were spaced out every five feet. Most of them were the same color as the bed frame, brown. The rug just in front of the bed and the one just inside the doorway were black.

"The bathroom is that way." Theoris said pointing to a corner of the room.

Hypatia carefully walked to it. She tried to walk in a straight line but only succeeded in tripping over one of the rugs.

Theoris watched Hypatia stagger across the floor with a growing arousal. Hypatia's wrap clung to her body and served only to heighten the feeling. Theoris walked over to a dresser and opened one shelf. She reached in and found a light cotton red gown. She walked over to the bathroom and heard Hypatia's grunted heaving into the toilet. She rapped softly on the door.

Hypatia lifted her head up from the toilet bowl. "Yes?" She said softly. "I'm okay." She heaved again.

Theoris slowly opened the door. "I brought you a night gown

to wear." She placed it on the sink. "I have an unopened toothbrush in the top sink drawer. Take all the time you need, okay?" She reached over and squeezed Hypatia's shoulder, back stepped quickly, and closed the door. She went back into the living room and retrieved the bottle of wine and the two glasses. She filled one glass and drank a mouth full down. She placed the glasses and wine on the dresser and went through one of the draws. A yellow sheer night gown was folded neatly on top of a folded pile of lingerie. She hummed to herself as she took off all her clothes and laid them over a chair. She walked the distance from the dresser to the living room but stopped in front of a full length mirror. She turned her backside to the mirror, looked at her rear end, and smiled. "Still looking good." She slipped the lingerie on and walked out the door. Theoris figured that Hypatia would be in the bathroom for a while. She decided to do a little work and go through her mail. The Message Carrier dropped her mail through a slot next to the door. She grabbed it, leafed through the lot, and tossed most of it in the trash. "Junk messages. Can't the Blessed Lands be free of junk messages?" She walked over to the living room couch and plopped herself down. The remote popped up out of one of the cushions. She switched on the AV and watched the news. After a moment of bad news she slipped into a relaxed sleep.

Hypatia couldn't remember when she passed out on the bathroom floor. She remembered Theoris saying something about an unopened toothbrush in the top drawer. After that things became a blur. Fortunately, Honey wine didn't give her a hangover. She counted on this and drank until she had more than her fill. After a moment of collected senses she pulled herself up to the sink. She looked in the mirror and saw her broken-veined bloodshot eyes. She giggled and reached into the top sink drawer and found the toothbrush. She also found a box of condoms, feminine napkins, and a tube of lubricant. She didn't want to know what it was used for. She brushed her teeth and thought about a shower or maybe even a bath. She decided neither and dressed in the gown Theoris had laid over the sink. Hypatia walked into the living room and noticed Theoris snoozing softly on the couch. She looked at the timepiece on the wall, 2:00 am. She walked over to the couch and lightly nudged Theoris' shoulder. Theoris woke up. She sat up rubbing her eyes. "Is it time to get dressed?"

Hypatia sat next to her. "No, it's two in the morning. You should be in bed. Come." She lifted Theoris and walked her into the bedroom. Both women sat on the bed.

Theoris said, "Feeling better?"

Hypatia nodded. "Yeah, much better." She looked around the room and spotted the two glasses and bottle of wine. She retrieved the bottle and two glasses, filled both up and handed one to Theoris. "You did say we had to finish it."

Theoris took the glass and drank a swallow. She reached out, touched Hypatia on the hand, and gave it a light squeeze.

Hypatia returned the favor. "You know, this afternoon I was so pissed at you."

Theoris nodded. "I can be a real bitch sometimes."

"Sometimes?"

Theoris laughed. "Most of the time. Sometimes I just forget to stop pushing so hard. Please forgive me. I know I came down heavy on you, but I couldn't stop thinking about the project. It really is very important to me."

Hypatia smiled and brushed a thicket of hair out of her face. She leaned in close and touched Theoris on the leg.

Theoris looked into Hypatia's eyes. "I don't want you to do anything you don't want to do."

Hypatia drained her glass. Theoris finished hers and handed it to Hypatia. Hypatia placed the glasses on the floor. She reached out and touched Theoris lightly on the cheek. "You're not making me do anything I don't want to do. It may surprise you but before Honute I was very much into women." She kissed her on the forehead.

Theoris smiled and kissed Hypatia on the lips, which tasted like toothpaste. She wrapped her arms around Hypatia's shoulders and moved her closer. She kissed her again and again - lightly and with affection. Hypatia returned the kisses and hugged Theoris hard. She pressed her lips close against Theoris' and slipped her tongue between the older woman's lips. Both women entwined themselves in a passionate embrace and collapsed on to the bed. Pillows were tossed to the floor and the bedspread was nearly torn as it was yanked down and away from the bed. Hypatia kissed Theoris' neck. She worked her way down to the shoulders, kissing and nibbling. Theoris moaned and crushed Hypatia's body into hers. Theoris slid her hand under Hypatia's gown and slipped them between her legs. She felt for the fold and lightly rubbed her hand up and down its length. Hypatia arched her back and moaned. It had been several weeks since her and Honute made love. Even when she was mad at him and indecisive whether to stay or leave she still looked forward to their love play. Honute had a way of bringing her to intense orgasms making her limp and putty in his arms. He delighted himself to the number of orgasms he could give her and almost always gave it his all. She did so with Theoris and planned on not sleeping until she had her screaming in ecstasy. She lifted Theoris' gown and licked her tongue over her stiffening nipple. Theoris' body trembled. It was the beginning of things to come.

Hypatia woke up to the sound of the alarm clock. It yanked her from a very blissful sleep. She dreamt that she had made love to Theoris for hours. Their bodies exhausted and covered in sweat from a passion that was deep and intoxicating. She looked over and saw Theoris groggily lift her head off the pillow and realized it wasn't a dream. Last night had been real. Hypatia reached over Theoris and hit the snooze button. She let her arm rest on her shoulder. "Doing okay?"

Theoris opened her eyes wide and smiled. "Yeah, I'm doing well." She leaned her head forward and gave Hypatia a kiss on the lips. Hypatia kissed back and before either of them realized the kissed turned passionate. Both women gave into the lust and explored each other, flicking and sliding their tongues against each other. They moved closer and gave into the longing desire to feel love and be loved. For the moment nothing mattered. The insistent sounding alarm clock accidentally knocked to the floor, forgotten. The telephone ring begging to be answered, forgotten. Their abandoned sensibilities to stop and get ready for work only added to the intensity of the moment and they simply and utterly gave into their bursting desire to have a final primordial orgastic symphony.

Chapter 10

Honute waited patiently for Theoris to show up. It was nearly ten o'clock when she finally did. Honute earlier, worried, had called the University. The campus operator recognized his voice and said that Dr. Hypatia had not arrived yet. Honute thought it strange but dismissed it. He remembered she told him that she would be sleeping at the University. It was a large place and maybe she was doing whatever she did somewhere else within the University. He thanked the operator and asked to be transferred to Dr. Theoris' office. The phone rang a half dozen times. Akila answered it and said Theoris wasn't in. She said she would call the Doctor's home number – "maybe she overslept?"

Maybe? Honute replied that he would wait by the phone, just in case. About an hour later, Theoris called and apologized for being late. She said that something unexpected came up and that she would be there as quickly as possibly. Another hour passed by the time the car pulled up to the cub in front of the apartment complex. Theoris blew the horn several times. To Honute she put a little too much into the horn. It sounded impatient and intense. Honute stepped out onto the balcony and waved at her. Theoris waved back and backed off the horn. He made his final check of the apartment, locked up, and went down the stairs. When Honute reached the car, the door thrust open. He stopped momentarily and peered inside. Theoris looked back with a serious look on her face. He stepped in and before he could close the door and put on his seatbelt she pulled away into traffic. He watched her from the corner of his eye. She remained mostly quiet but he sensed something wrong. It was as if today she was a different person or she had a different attitude toward him. "How are you doing this morning?"

Theoris was lost in thought when Honute asked her how she was doing. Her stomach knotted up for a brief moment. She answered with her jaw clinched tight. "Fine, why?"

Honute cocked his head to one side. "I was worried. I just wanted to know if you are doing well."

She nodded and stared out the windshield. "I am well. I just had a long night."

Honute nodded and remained quiet for the rest of the trip.

Hypatia was looking out the window when she saw Theoris pulled the car into the stall next to her's. She had been waiting anxiously. After their morning love making Hypatia felt a little guilty. She betrayed Honute and neither said much during the time it took for both to get ready for work. The silence was only really broken after they showered together and gotten dressed. Theoris asked what Hypatia wanted to do. Hypatia said she needed to think about this. She hadn't meant for any of this to happen, but since it did happen she needed to make a decision. Theoris kissed her on the forehead and asked would she be staying the night again. Hypatia surprised herself and nodded. They kissed each other and left – Theoris to pick up Honute, Hypatia to work.

When the car pulled into the stall Hypatia's stomach knotted up and a lump formed in her throat. She watched as her husband of many years and her new lover of just as many hours walk into the building. She shook her head and thought about the mess she just got herself into.

Theoris pulled into the stall and suddenly her face grew dark.

Honute felt more than saw the sudden change and decided that he didn't want to know what was going on. His gut told him to let it lie, he wouldn't like the answer anyway.

Theoris sat for a moment before turning off the engine. She noticed Honute watching patiently. He only made a move for the door when she did. She stepped out he stepped out. She closed the door he closed the door. He stared back, grinned, and followed her inside. He remained silent but kept a distance from the time they entered the building all the way to the time they both walked through the door to the main office.

Akila had been pacing impatiently when Theoris and Honute walked in. She looked up and simply said, "Dr. Theoris, good afternoon. Hello Priest Honute."

Theoris nodded and walked by. "I'll be in my office, give me about ten minutes."

"Yes, Dr. Theoris." Akila said to the receding Doctor. She turned to Honute who had been standing just inside the doorway. "May I get you something to drink, Honute? Bark tea?"

"Akila, that would be nice, thank you." Honute said and found his way to the couch.

Hypatia nearly jumped when the phone rang. She answered it on the fourth ring. "Hypatia speaking, hello?" She heard Theoris' voice and grinned.

"Hypatia, how are you doing?"

"I'm doing okay. It is good to hear your voice."

"What are you doing right now?"

Hypatia giggled. "Waiting for you to get to work and let me know you were in."

Theoris laughed at herself. Hypatia made her feel twenty years younger. She hadn't been this happy in a while. Then she thought about Honute.

Hypatia heard the laugh and felt good, and then she heard nothing and nearly panicked. "What's the matter?"

Theoris sighed. "Nothing. What are you doing at two?"

Hypatia leafed through her calendar. "Nothing, however, I got a meeting at 3:30. You want to come over?"

Theoris nodded and said, "Yeah, I do. I'll bring us something to eat. Will you be able to hold out that long?"

"I will. See you in a few hours."

Both said their good-byes.

Theoris walked out her office and saw Honute and Akila sitting on the couch chatting.

Akila sat leaning back on the armrest, sipping tea, smiling at Honute.

He said something that apparently amused her and she reached out and touched him on the arm. He blushed, took a sip of tea and said something else.

Akila laughed and then noticed Theoris.

Theoris frowned and said, "Are you two quite enjoying yourselves?"

Akila looked at Theoris for several seconds. "Is there something the matter Dr. Theoris? You wanted us to wait for you? Correct?"

Theoris thought about saying something to her assistant but decided not to. Her mood just turned bad and she didn't know why. She was going to have lunch with her new lover, which ought to have kept her happy. She stared at Honute. He stared back with the same intensity, then she realized why she was in a foul mood. She lightened her expression and forced a smile. Honute smoothly smiled back, but kept his eyes even. Theoris was screwing his wife and the man didn't have a clue. She then realized that she was mad at herself. She seduced Hypatia. Now their affair would eventually complicate things because things like sleeping with another person's spouse never stayed a secret forever. She sighed, "I am sorry, Akila, Honute. I am just in a bad mood. Please forgive me."

Honute nodded. "You don't seem to be a religious person, Theoris. Otherwise I would offer you prayer to ease your mind."

Theoris was nearly mortified. The thought of her being blessed sounded ridiculous at best. "No, thank you. It is okay." She hoped that it came out civil.

"Okay," Honute said nodding, "Then maybe someone to talk too. I am licensed as a Listener."

Theoris paused for a moment. Listeners had to go through years of schooling, nearly a decade. And Honute offered to 'listen.' Just one more thing about him that made him likable. Theoris cursed her gonads for being the dominant brain. "Um, thank you,

Honute, maybe I will consider it. I guess that the offer has been presented makes me feel better." It didn't but as a Listener he would have to set aside all prejudices and she figured it would be her 'get out of jail card' when the time came to confess.

Honute bowed.

Theoris cleared her throat. "Okay, I suppose we should get started. Akila, Honute, follow me to my office. I'll outline everything from there."

Akila nodded and followed Honute and Theoris into her office.

Theoris gave Honute a clipboard with a small thick stack of papers. "I'll need you to read through each sheet and initial at the bottom. Three of the forms require signatures."

Honute took the clipboard and sat in an upholstered chair in front of the desk. The first form was a non-disclosure agreement. He was supposed to keep quiet on how Theoris achieved her goal. He initialed it. The second form was an agreement that he would not sue the Doctor or the University in the event that something unforeseen happened. Like him losing eyes, limbs, or the function of any appendage including the all important penile one. He initialed that one too. He did this with every form. Some amused him. Like the one that read he was of sound mind and body and that Theoris, her staff, and the University waived all claims to erroneous visions that may or may not result in some of the medication he may or may not receive. He initialed them all and signed the three forms he had to. He handed the clipboard back to Theoris.

She took the board and placed it in a drawer in her desk. "Excellent." She said and leaned back in her chair. "The first thing we are going to do today is get a baseline of your physiological and psychological properties. Akila will handle the physiological part."

Honute nodded. So far he understood.

Theoris continued, "Once that is done we'll start the program. Hopefully this time tomorrow you'll be hooked up to a bunch of wires, attached to a dozen machines, resting in a bed."

"How long will all this take?" Honute asked.

"Maybe a month, maybe two, three and four at the most. I very seriously doubt longer than that. If we get no results by that time then my reasoning and all the data collected is wrong."

"Under normal circumstances I wouldn't care, but since pay was mentioned, how much will I receive?"

Theoris smiled. She possibly had an 'advance to go' card. "For the moment, one hundred fifty a week."

Honute frowned. "I suppose I should be thankful I'm getting that much. May I have an advance, say two months worth?"

Theoris' eyebrows drew together

"I only ask for the advance because my pay will not cover next month's rent. Hypatia's income alone paid the rent. I'll have to figure something out about the utilities. A prayer to Thoth might help, but you can imagine the landlord probably not accepting blessings for rent." Honute smiled.

Akila nodded and smiled.

Theoris tried to conceal her discomfort. The pay was actually five hundred a week, but for some reason she told him one hundred fifty. Anger? She shook her head. Jealousy maybe.

"Maybe half then." Honute said.

Theoris realized he took her head shaking as a denial to his request.

"I'm sorry, Honute, I wasn't shaking my head to your request, I was . . . it doesn't matter. I'll see what I can do." She was finding it difficult to hate Honute. Basically, he seemed to be a victim of circumstances. He lost his wife and will probably lose his shelter. The irony of it all was that she was sleeping with his wife who just happened to receive a thirty percent increase in pay. Money and shelter were the least of Hypatia's concerns. Theoris re-iterated. "I'll see what I can do." The knot in her stomach got harder and bigger.

Chapter 11

Honute rested on the bed. On one side of him was an EKG machine and on the other side was an EEG machine. He had wires draped across his legs, lap, arms, and chest. Both machines beeped every other second. "I'm supposed to relax, right?"

Akila stood over the EKG machine. Honute's heart pattern readout on a small CRT in the standard Rhythm II wave – PQRST. She tapped at several buttons on the machine's small keypad. The readout displayed his Rhythm II wave. She tapped out a few more commands and the screen displayed recording. "Yes, you're supposed to relax." She walked over to the EEG machine and repeated the process of viewing a few patterns and then set the machine to record mode. "I'll be back in sixty minutes. Think some good thoughts." She brushed her hand across his shoulder.

Honute inhaled and exhaled deeply. He counted from one hundred to zero, but got sidetracked numerous times. He had to restart three times and for some reason he could not get passed the number sixty-nine. Then he decided to think about Akila. She was wearing a tan colored wrap today. The material wasn't as sheer as her white cotton one, but it hugged her body in the usual and important places. He started to get a hard-on and blushed. He wondered what type of readings the machines were getting. He thought about his duties back at the temple and wondered who was filling in for him. Priest Anguliko was good and motivated, but he doubted Head Priest Guriamon would pull him from his missionary duties. Priest Yurikaki could do his job, but he was new. Honute closed his eyes and he saw Akila's face shining at him. He snapped his eyes open and saw Akila looking at him.

"Honute, you're supposed to be relaxing. Now relax, okay?"

Honute nodded and closed his eyes again. He imagined Akila in his arms and the two of them sitting on the beach looking out at the descending sun. He liked this dream. He imagined the softness of her skin against his and traced his imaginary finger down the length of her imaginary leg. He snapped his eyes opened and tried to relax again. He watched Akila walk away with a smile on her face.

Akila walked away blushing. She noticed Honute had a rather large bulge between his legs. She doubted that whatever he was thinking was relaxing him. Quite the opposite really. She smiled to herself as she walked back into the main computer room. Secretly, she hoped that she was the reason for the bulge.

Hypatia sat at her desk looking at Theoris. Both women finished eating lunch. Theoris walked in holding a bag of take-out from one of the local vendors. She liked the one that was just outside the entrance way to the University. The roadside kitchen was almost always crowded and that's what made it appealing. She walked up and ordered a dozen mutton and lamb kebabs. She also made sure that several large slices of flatbread and a skinned onion cut in two were included.

Theoris gathered up the empty wrappers and used napkins and placed everything in the trash basket. She handed Hypatia a stick of breath saving gum. "How'd you like the lunch?" She asked.

Hypatia placed the stick of gum in her mouth and chewed. "It was very good. Almost as good as . . . ." She paused for a second. "It was very good. I've never eaten there before."

Theoris nodded. "It's one of my favorites."

Both women stared at one another. Seconds ticked by and the silence seemed almost unbearably.

Theoris said, "Hypatia, I should never assume anything, but do you still love Honute?"

Hypatia frowned and turned away. "I do love him, but I'm not in love with him, and I don't plan on changing my mind about the divorce." She turned back. "That is what you are asking? Will I change my mind and go back to him after we begin a relationship, which I'm assuming you want."

Theoris thought for a moment. She nodded. "Yes, I would like to pursue a possible relationship with you."

Hypatia said, "Pursue a possible relationship?"

"Yes, are we compatible enough to eventually get passed the physical attraction?"

Hypatia thought Theoris a pretty woman for her age, but not a beautiful woman. Sex was good, but not perfectly great. Hypatia enjoyed the feeling of a real penis sliding back and forth between her legs, not plastic or even simulated flesh. The real thing was just that – the real thing. Hypatia considered Theoris' personality. She liked the way Theoris carried herself with confidence and self-assuredness. And that she was very influential – which was a very powerful aphrodisiac, but she wanted that in a man. Then there was Theoris' sometimes abusive and intimidating side. If she were a male it would have been called 'competitive, go-getting, assertive and commanding' but for a female it was simply called 'being a bitch!' "We did do this rather sudden."

"I'd like you to spend the night again. I could have some food delivered. Maybe rent several RAVs."

Hypatia nodded slowly and smiled. She really didn't have a place to go nor did she have a good reason to decline the invitation. It seemed prudent to follow through with the situation. "I'd like that." She said simply.

A great weight seemed to lift off Theoris' shoulders. She really hadn't considered what she would have done if Hypatia rejected her offer. Her last lover was a male intern. He was six feet five inches and a part-time dancer. She had him for two years and loved ever single day. Though he was moderately ambitious he couldn't handle to riggers of multi-disciplinary science. In the end he decided to get the Master's degree and become a full-time dancer. To this day he sends her a birthday and Christmas card and invites her to all his performances when he is in or near New Heliopolis. Theoris got up and walked over to Hypatia. She reached into her skirt pocket and pulled out a key. "It's to the front door. Here."

Hypatia took the key and held it.

Theoris leaned down and kissed Hypatia on the forehead. She turned and walked out the office and headed back across the street.

Hypatia looked at the key and wondered how much accepting it was going to cost her. She turned her chair around to face the window and watched Theoris walk into the building across the street. She looked at the key again and likened it to the keys of the underworld. A door twice locked is never once opened.

Chapter 12

The LIN train glided smoothly to a stop in front of New Heliopolis' main passenger transfer hub. Ferruk and Ayruyi stood up and walked toward the private exit. Two of his bodyguards were waiting just outside the train. The other two would cover the rear. Ferruk's position gave him access to first class accommodations to nearly all modes of transportation in the Blessed Lands. The Royal family and the Continental Vizier had priority over his claim. So, whenever Ferruk did travel he made sure no one more important than he would be within a hundred mile radius.

Trujin and Fugyar, his main bodyguard's surveyed the area with the precision of military experts. Trujin touched his hand to his collar and spoke. He signaled Guyren and Ivoniyut, the rear guards that everything was clear. A moment later Ferruk and Ayruyi emerged from the train. A long black motor vehicle pulled up and everyone entered.

Ferruk told the driver to head to New Heliopolis Hotel. The journey had been long and he wanted to avail himself to the pleasures of Ayruyi before he visited Dr. Theoris.

Theoris entered the little office where Akila was monitoring Honute. "How is the recording and monitoring? Does it look like we'll get a good baseline?"

Akila looked up from one of the monitor screens. "Anything is going well Doctor. Honute is in extraordinarily good physical shape. His EEG shows a well balanced psyche and the EKG shows he has a very strong heart. I had Dr. Hyowen's group collect blood samples earlier. We should get a complete chart by tomorrow morning."

"Excellent, Akila." Theoris said. She looked at the young woman and wondered what she was thinking. Of course, the easiest and most obvious way to find out was to just ask. But in asking she might give, in way of a clue, what the question was really getting at. Theoris looked around and pretended to study several of the monitors. She tapped on the keyboard in front of one of the monitors. A small graphic window popped up. It displayed a real-time wire graph of Honute's mental state. Six different colored lines squiggled and wiggled on the display. Theoris tapped on the keyboard again. One of the colored lines, light blue, became prominent. Text readout scrolled along side the line. "Akila?" Theoris asked. "Have you been studying the EEG?"

Akila handed Theoris a folder. "Doctor, it is amazing. He is in a deep meditative state. His delta waves are at zero point five cps."

"Zero point five? Amazing! How long did it take for him to reach that?"

Akila smiled. "Less than a minute. That is less than a minute after he had an erotica episode."

Theoris looked up from the graph nestled in the folder. "An erotica episode? Do you know the reason for it?" She quickly looked Akila up and down and hoped.

Akila blushed and smiled. "I think so." She turned her attention to a monitor and acted like she found a squiggly line intriguing.

Theoris sat next to Akila and leaned in close. She whispered as if the room were full of ease droppers – they were the only two in the room. "Was it you?"

Akila blushed deepened. "I think so."

"Really? What made you think so?"

Akila giggled. "After I finished hooking him up I brushed my hand across his chest. It was an accident but after it happened the EEG read an increase in his Beta waves. They jumped from seventeen to thirty-two. When I told him to relax and think of something pleasant his theta waves hit five cps and beta disappeared. He had a hard on, so I know it was something arousing."

Theoris smiled. "What do you think about him?"

Akila looked at Theoris. "Think about him? In what way?"

Theoris laughed, this was beginning to be the best day of her life. "Do you like him?"

Akila looked away. "I suppose so. He seems intriguing enough, but he's married and a priest."

"Neither of which precludes him from having a relationship. Besides, he is getting a divorce."

"I don't know . . ." Akila trailed off.

"When I left you two alone yesterday, I went to talk to Dr. Hypatia, his wife."

Akila gasped.

"I confronted her and asked if Honute being part of the research was going to be a problem."

Akila was nearly horrified. She didn't think she would have been bold enough to do such a thing, but Dr. Theoris' directness was one of the reasons she admired her.

"Dr. Hypatia", Theoris began, "assured me that there would be no issues."

"That's good." Akila said.

Theoris nodded. "So, if you feel inclined to see how far and deep his feelings are, I encourage it."

Akila frowned. Dr. Theoris had been a firm believer in keeping research and relationships separate.

"I know in the past that I've stressed the separation of business and pleasure, particularly with research subjects, but in this case – Priest Honute seems like a genuine gentleman, I don't see a reason to not pursue it. Beside, you'll be able to see and possibly notice minute changes by being close to him."

Akila nodded but decided to give Theoris' words careful thought and consideration. The fact that the Doctor so much as blessed a relationship gave reason to be very suspicious. Theoris never did anything unless it had an end purpose to her means. "I'll think about it Dr. Theoris."

Theoris smiled. "Good." She then stood up and looked out the door and saw Honute stretched out on the bed. She would have thought all the wires running across his chest, arms and legs would be very uncomfortable but he seemed, and the EEG machine confirmed, that he was not bothered in the least. She turned back to Akila. "How long has it been?"

"About an hour of good recording time. I was going to run the full ninety minutes."

Theoris nodded. "Excellent, I'll be in my office in the mean time. Bring Honute when everything is done."

Akila simply said, "Yes, Doctor."

Theoris left and walked to her office. Just outside her door stood two brawny men dressed in black. When she was close enough to be heard with yelling she asked, "What are you doing in front of my office?"

One of the two men, Trujin, looked at her. "Dr. Theoris, please forgive our intrusion. Head Priest of the Middle Lands, Vizier of the Area for Pharaoh, Friend to the Royal Family, Ferruk is waiting for you."

Theoris' face twisted up in a nasty and frightening look of anger, fear, and pain. "What in the underworld is he doing here?" And she pushed her door opened. She stepped in. Ferruk and a young lady sat on the office couch and two more security men stood on either side of the couch looking like bookends.

Before Theoris could launch herself in a tirade Ferruk swiftly and smoothly rose. "My daringly Theoris, my how beautiful you still look to my eyes. I am so sorry I hadn't called ahead of time but I find that my visit is very important. Can we talk?"

Theoris gave Ferruk a piercing stare and walked around to her desk. She surveyed the contents on it as if she was able to discern any tampering. "What do you want?"

Ferruk's look of hurt would have been priceless to Theoris if she thought it genuine. "You mean I can't socialize with you first?"

"No."

"Theoris, I am hurt . . ."

"Just get to the point and leave. This time make the in between visits longer."

Ferruk checked his temper and smiled congenially. Theoris was still beautiful to him and he did miss her. He occasionally followed her career and was pleased when he first heard that she because a Friend to Pharaoh and the Royal family. He never contacted her directly because of their bitter breakup, what a long long time ago. It was probably approaching twenty years and the last time they saw each other was perhaps ten. "Very well, then. My future is in your hands and I must know how and what you are currently doing."

"What I'm doing?"

Ferruk nodded, "Yes, the Oracle foretold a future . . ."

Theoris laughed out loud.

Ferruk was taken aback by Theoris' outburst. "You think that funny?"

Theoris wiped a tear from her eye and settled her laughter to a chuckle. "Yeah, that is funny. When have you let someone else tell you your future? The mighty Ferruk worried about his next meal."

Ferruk snapped, "Who said I was worried?"

"It's all over your face! What am I suppose to think? You travel all this distance with your thugs and this . . . this eye candy." She gestured toward Ayruyi.

"She is one of my servants."

"No doubt." Theoris looked Ayruyi up and down. "You fuck her, don't you?"

Ferruk snapped again, "That's none of your business how I handle my servants. I'm quite good to them actually." It sounded high and mighty and not very convincing.

Ayruyi's expression darkened for a moment. It took her a few seconds to recover and lighten her features.

Theoris caught the expression and regretted what she said. Even though servants had rights in the Blessed Lands it was not the same as being a fully vested citizen. Ferruk could do almost anything he liked to her. Anything short of maim and murder and if he did do such a thing he would have to face an inquiry of peers, not prison. The worst punishment Theoris heard that had been handed down to an abusive master was a hefty fine and the lost of servants for ten years. Hardly a damaging sentence for killing one's keeps. She pressed her lips together and sat down. "What did this Oracle say?"

Chapter 13

Akila walked into the room and gently called Honute's name. She shook him lightly. "Honute, you can wake up now. I've finished recording." She started removing the alligator clips from the many electro-contacts along his chest, shoulders, calves, forehead and neck.

Honute opened his eyes and smiled. "All done?"

Akila nodded. "You have an excellent ability to go into a deep trance."

Honute stretched and placed his loose fitting shirt back on. "Hours of prayer can do that I guess. May I be able to see some of the readout? I've never seen what a trance looks like on paper."

Akila answered certainly. She walked him into the control room and sat him at a desk. She flipped a switch on a monitor and the screen sparkled on. She tapped at the keyboard in front of him.

Honute found himself mesmerized by Akila's presence. She was close enough for him to smell the perfume she was wearing. It smelled of Nile air and lotus blossoms with a hint of honey. It reminded him of Hypatia's fragrance, but it had a slightly different smell. Then he frowned and wondered what Hypatia was doing this moment. Was she thinking about him?

Akila noticed the frown. "Honute, is something wrong?"

He looked up. "No, not really."

"Is there anything I can do? Do you want to talk?"

His lips thinned out as he pressed them together. "I don't know how appropriate it would be." He shook his head. "No, everything is fine, really."

Akila slowly said, "Okay, but if you need to talk. I'm here. Okay?"

He nodded and smiled. Then said, "Is this me in a deep trance?"

Akila laughed softly. She had the graph up when he had an erotic episode, more of a thought actually, but he didn't need to know that. "No, this was when you were thinking about something that got you agitated. It could have been the thought of anything."

"Really?" Honute looked worried. "This machine can read thoughts?"

Akila shook her head, "No, not at all. And maybe that was a good thing."

Honute laughed nervously, not completely convinced that the machine hadn't caught him with his pants down.

"Really, Honute. The machine, in this case, the EEG machine only picks up brain signals."

"Okay." Honute said.

"Here." She pointed to a spot on the screen. "This pattern is called Beta waves. It occurs when a person is awake and conscious of the surrounding world. You became intensely aware of something, right here, then after several minutes you relaxed into an Alpha state."

Honute looked at the squiggly wiggly lines. He squinted thinking that maybe the lines would make better sense. They didn't and he opened his eyes wide. He wondered what type of wave pattern he would be generating now. Akila's aroma was deeply satisfying.

"During Alpha state, a person is relaxed. Usually day dreaming happens here. It's the start of mediation. And this point is when you enter Theta state. It normally occurs when a person is dreaming or has a deep connection with the sub-conscious mind. Divine inspiration has been known to come out of Theta state."

Honute nodded. He was beginning to see the patterns now. "And this line?" It was long and sinuous.

"Deep sleep. And if you notice, just after it there is a

combination of states. You started mediating here. The only reason I know you were not awake is the absence of Beta waves."

"You can really tell? Fascinating."

"It is fascinating." Akila answered.

"What other tests will I have to go through?"

"Well, tonight we'll have to do another baseline recording."

"Another one?"

Akila nodded, "Yeah. Your sleep patterns. I'll have to stay up most of the night and monitor the equipment."

Honute frowned. "That won't be any fun. Watching me sleep."

Akila just smiled and shrugged.

"I'll have to sleep in these clothes? Can I go home and get a change?"

"I'll ask Dr. Theoris if she could run you home. . ."

Honute thought about this morning's encounter. "Maybe I can catch a cab. I really don't want to burden Dr. Theoris with such a simple task." Akila smiled again and Honute loved it. His gaze locked on her full lips and he nearly stammered. "M-maybe, I don't have to go home. I just need some place to wash up."

"We have a bathroom, with shower, down the hall. I use it sometimes when I have to work late."

"Will you be getting any sleep?" Honute asked.

"Some, but don't you worry about me. I'm a night owl! I've stayed up for nearly forty-eight hours working on school reports and student papers. It's nothing."

Honute looked into Akila eyes and felt guilty that he stopped thinking about Hypatia. But the fact was they had drifted apart months ago and the connection had been lost between the two of them long before that.

Akila looked at her watch. "Oh, we should head down to Dr. Theoris' office. She wanted to see the two of us." She headed for the door.

Honute got up and happily followed. He wondered which combination of waves would appear now. He intently watched Akila's slim frame walk gracefully down the hall.

Ferruk sat on the couch. He turned to Ayruyi and commanded, "Get us some coffee."

Theoris appalled said, "No, you will not!"

Ayruyi stopped.

Ferruk turned to Theoris and said, "Please allow my servant to perform her duties."

Theoris jumped up and nearly ran toward Ferruk. Ivoniyut stuck out an arm and blocked her from getting any closer. Theoris screamed, "How dare you display you chauvinist ways in my office."

Ferruk stood up. He leaned close to Theoris and said, "My bodyguards are trained to react with deadly force. Please don't rush up on me again." He sat down and turned to Ayruyi again. "Get us some coffee now!"

Ayruyi hurried out.

Akila rounded the corner to the main hallway toward Dr. Theoris' office and nearly collided into a young woman. The woman wore the traditional attire marking her as a slave.

"Excuse me." Ayruyi said winded. "But could you please show me were I may be able to get coffee for my master?"

Akila's face contorted into a mixture of shame and anger. She had a severe disdain regarding slavery. For all the good things within the Blessed Lands servitude was not one of them. Akila felt a bit of pity toward the young lady, but there wasn't much she could do about her captivity. Servitude was protected under the Blessed Laws given to the people by Pharaoh. "Coffee? I can show you. Where are you coming from?"

Ayruyi bowed. "Thank you. From Dr. Theoris' Office."

Honute stepped up next to Akila.

"Dr. Theoris is my boss. We," Akila pointed to Honute and herself, "were going there."

Honute frowned when he realized the young woman was a servant.

Ayruyi saw Honute and bowed deeply. "Priest personage."

Honute bent his head in a bow. "What is your name?"

"Ayruyi, good priest."

"Call me Honute, please, and not so formal." Then he turned to Akila. "I didn't know Theoris had a servant."

Akila replied, "She doesn't."

"Oh."

Ayruyi spoke up. "My master is Ferruk, Head Priest of the Middle Lands, Vizier of the Area for Pharaoh, Friend to the Royal Family. He is here to speak of important matters with Dr. Theoris."

Honute's eyes widened. "The holy priest of the Area is here?"

Ayruyi nodded and said with as much impatience in her voice as she dared show in the presence of a priest. "My master has requested coffee for all present. I would be most grateful for your assistance."

Akila nodded and said. "Ayruyi, follow me. I can help."

Ayruyi looked relieved and bowed deeply. She followed Akila and Honute into the large office.

Theoris' expression turned ugly. Her gazed pierced deep into Ferruk. She stepped back. "You know, I changed my mind."

"Oh really? In what way?" Ferruk asked.

Theoris turned and sat at her chair. "I could care less why you are here. Take your cinder heads and your slave and leave."

Ferruk laughed.

Theoris' temperature rose a degree for each second Ferruk chuckled to himself.

"It's not that simple, Theoris."

"The hell it is not. You stand up and walk out. The door is to your right."

Ferruk leaned forward. "You're making this difficult, you know that?"

"I'm about to make it impossible in a few minutes. This is my office, which . . ."

". . . which is part of my University, Dr. Theoris." Said the Chairman of the University, Dr. Pilboluti. Dr. Jeyrulis, the president of the University was a half step behind him. Pilboluti continued, "Vizier Ferruk. Please forgive Dr. Theoris. She misunderstood you I am sure. Her research is completely and absolutely open to you."

Ferruk bowed his head slightly. "I admit that I did not get a chance to explain to Dr. Theoris that Pharaoh, through me, supports her research."

The two University officials beamed and bowed deeply. Pilboluti stepped over to Theoris and handed her a letter.

Theoris thought about ripping the letter to shreds but common sense and a notion of civility squelched that urge. She read it. It was an official letter from the offices of Pharaoh and it left the Vizier of the Middle area to observe the research and report as Vizier saw fit to report research. Theoris looked up. She felt nearly defeated.

Pilboluti smiled widely and said, "Now that everyone is in agreement that Vizier Ferruk is to be an observer for His almighty and most exalted Pharaoh who is incarnate of Ra, most powerful deity of the heavens, we may get down to work."

There was silence for a moment. Theoris handed the letter back to Pilboluti, who took it, folded it, and placed it in his coat pocket. She turned to the doorway.

Ayruyi, Akila, and Honute entered the office each holding a tray of coffee, tea, and date cakes. Ayruyi placed the tray on a table off to one side of the office. She picked up a cup and saucer and walked it over to Ferruk. He took it, tasted it, and nodded. Ayruyi quietly sat next to him. Akila served the two bodyguards and Honute gave cups to Pilboluti and Jeyrulis. He then gave Theoris a cup of tea. She thanked him and he bowed slightly.

Theoris took a sip of tea and said. "Gentlemen, this is Priest Honute. He has volunteered to help us out in the research."

Honute turned and bowed to Pilboluti and Jeyrulis. They each returned the gesture. He then turned to Ferruk and bowed deeply.

"Most High Priest, I am one of your simple servants, giving praise and salvation to the populace in the Landful district of New Heliopolis." He stood up.

Ferruk had been sipping his tea when Honute bowed and gave the introductory of a lesser priest in the presence of a superior. Ferruk placed the cup down at the same time Honute stood up. He nearly dropped the cup. In the twenty years of being a priest in the circles of powerful people Ferruk never once lost his composure or demeanor. Today was the closest he had. "May Ra, Osiris, and Isis guide you through his living journey. From what temple do you give praise to?"

Honute thought he noticed something off from Ferruk. It unnerved him for a second, but he regained proper deportment and slipped into the familiar posture of a lesser priest addressing a superior. "Thoth, Temple of Science, Reasoning and Thinking, honored Priest Ferruk."

Ferruk acknowledged Honute.

Theoris took the whole scene in with disgust. The whole notion of male posturing smacked at her sensibilities as silly and wasteful.

Akila watched disturbed but managed to look indifferent.

Ayruyi just watched. This was nothing new to her. Ferruk demanded lesser priest give him due respect. She was relieved that Honute was spared the extreme indignities Ferruk can put on an inferior.

Ferruk turned to Theoris. "Now that we have an understanding. I will leave you to your work. I've assigned my routine and public functionary duties to my assistant. Everything else that is important I will handle down here for the remainder of your project, Dr. Theoris."

Theoris grunted and begrudgingly nodded. "Shall we meet each morning or would a daily report emailed be to your satisfaction?" She hoped the latter would be to his liking.

"A daily report would be best and we can meet each Tuesday. We are entering the cycle of Bast and Tuesday would be most appropriate."

Theoris nodded again.

Ferruk stepped away from the couch and walked toward the door. One bodyguard was on the other side surveying the area and the other lingered back a little. He would effectively cover Ferruk's retreat. Ayruyi would pace herself behind Ferruk. He turned, nodded to everyone and left.

After a moment Theoris turned to Pilboluti. "We'll talk later, when I've had a chance to calm down."

Pilboluti nodded and walked out. Theoris' words sank in and by the time he reached the doorway his posture was that of a beaten man ready for his punishment.

Jeyrulis followed silently.

Honute and Akila remained quiet.

Theoris turned to Honute and didn't say a word. His pitiful actions angered her still. On one level she knew it wasn't his fault. It was the nature of his position. And besides, his behavior demonstrated the very reason he was a good candidate. It was on the other level of gut feeling that his actions sickened her. He dropped several niches on her measuring stick. She slowly tore her gaze from Honute and looked at Akila. "I have an engagement to attend to. I will leave you to finish up with today's measurements. Tomorrow we'll plot the baseline and begin with stimuli testing."

Akila nodded.

Theoris switched her computer off and walked out the door.

Honute stood watching as she walked out. He turned to Akila. "I don't suppose I'm to know what just happened?"

Akila had also been deeply disturbed. She slowly shook her head several times. "No, you're not expected to."

Honute nodded and felt somewhat better. He considered blessing the room with a prayer but decided against it. Something important happened today and he missed most of it. He looked at Akila and saw a bit of coldness in her eyes. Her warmth had vanished and that was a tragedy. He would bless the room tomorrow.

Akila wasn't sure whether she was mad at Honute, Ferruk, or herself. Theoris had been her mentor and teacher for a few years now and she admired the woman greatly. She saw her as a role model and poster child for independent liberal minded women. For Ferruk to walk in with an obvious submissive servant was one thing, but to watch Honute bow out as the dominate male was another. The scene tore at her heart and left her with mixed feelings.

On an intellectual level she understood Honute's and Ferruk's interplay. It was vital for the continued insurance of the established hierarchy of priesthood. But in her summation, short years as an adult and teachings handed down from Dr. Theoris, it still stank.

On the emotional level, however, the feelings were somewhat different. She was beginning to fall for Honute and that bothered her. The fact was he didn't look the part of a priest. There was something about him that contradicted his complacent meekness. The way he firmly placed his feet on the ground had a finality that would give Ra pause in moving him. The way his biceps, deltoids, and triceps flexed underneath his tunic sleeves. And when he walked his body moved with a gracefulness that rivaled many in Pharaoh's Royal Dancing Troupe. The man's body screamed warrior and alpha, but his demeanor and personality shouted beta and subservient. He was just one total dichotomy of meek and brawn.

Chapter 14

Theoris and Akila sat in the smaller office while Honute was left alone in Theoris' office. Akila seemed uneasy. She swayed side to side from nervous tension. Theoris paced the length of the office. "I'm not liking how this is developing."

Akila nodded in silence.

"Ferruk breathing down my neck is unacceptable." Theoris said. "If this project wasn't so important I'd sabotage it." She looked over to Akila and stopped pacing.

Akila stared back.

"Don't worry. We'll have to deal with this professionally." She started pacing again. After several moments she stopped and turned to Akila again. "What do you think of Honute?"

"Doctor, what exactly do you mean?"

"What are your feelings about him? Your gut feeling?"

Akila stopped swaying and pondered for a moment. She was having emotional feelings for him, but she didn't think it appropriate to have them or even voice her feelings to Theoris. Akila assumed that the Doctor meant first impressions and objective observations. "I think he is a nice guy. He seems to really like his job and the short time I have been able to chat with him has been very pleasant."

Theoris nodded solemnly. "But what are your feelings for him?"

Akila blushed.

"My young prodigy, I have watched you around him. You're feelings are a bit transparent."

Akila blushed deeply and for an instant was mad. Theoris had seen through her veil. She really tried hard to keep anything clinical and on the surface, but apparently, at some point, her deep feelings buoyed to the surface. "I like him and I find him intriguing. He is a dichotomy." There, she said it.

Theoris stood in silence for a few moments. She nodded after a time and said, "Yes." Then she asked, "How were you affected by this afternoon?"

Akila replied. "A little bit hurt, more angry. I wasn't sure if it was at Priest Ferruk for posturing around us or at Honute for being in the position of having to be postured at. I was embarrassed for him and that kind of pissed me off."

Theoris nodded again. "Yes, that display nagged at my sensibilities. Do you think Honute is right for this research?"

Akila cocked her head to one side. "Right? As in perfect subject?"

"Right as in, right person to give this ability."

Akila thought for a moment. "I don't know. I don't know enough of Honute to know how he will react. I can only guess at how it will change him mentally, if there is a change."

Theoris stood silent.

"I had requested a search in the repository for some background data on Honute. It came in but I hadn't had a chance to look at it. I had it saved to my Inbox."

"Really? May I look at it?"

Akila nodded. "Of course, Dr. Theoris. I'll bring it up on the system?"

Theoris nodded.

Akila sat at the desk and tapped away on the keyboard. She frowned. "It's asked me for a login and pass code." She tapped something out. "Mine doesn't work."

Theoris walked to the desk. "Let's try mine." And she typed out her login and code she used to access her office computer. After a second hesitation she hit the enter key.

Theoris held her breath as the document decompressed and opened. It intrigued her that a mere humble priest's records would be encoded. Akila's access clearance was high enough to access anything she needed to perform her duties and research. That should have included opening a regular citizen of the Blessed Lands' dossier. The document opened up and a splash page with the Royal Family's seal was on it. At the bottom read the statement that only authorized individuals of the Blessed Lands could read this without prosecution and threat of death. Theoris swallowed hard. Akila's swallow was just as audible. She tapped the page down button on the keyboard. The next page had a brief bio and photo of Honute. He looked considerably younger and he had a disarming smile. It was hard to tell how long ago the photo was taken, but the youthful lack of lines, smoothness in his skin, and the shine in his eyes was enough to guess at least twenty years ago. Both women looked at each other for a brief moment and went back to reading. The bio stated that Honute had served with honors in Pharaoh's Royal Army. He had twelve tours of duties against the Peoples of the Cursed Land across Ra's Resting Ocean. He was highly decorated and received Pharaoh's Scarab on three different occasions. Theoris couldn't remember a time that the Scarab was awarded to anyone alive. Now, she had a war hero sitting in her office. "This changes a few things." She said out loud.

Akila had been reading the bio but could hardly understand that the Honute-now was the same Honute-then. Her stomach knotted up as she tried to make sense of the whole thing. "Doctor, what could have happened to him?"

Theoris shook her head slowly. "I don't know. He is clearly someone special." She tapped the page down button several times. A page titled INTREGRATION came up. Both women scanned the page quickly. It was amazing Theoris thought. Honute had survived until retirement, but because of the nature of his background had to undergo extensive and intensive behavior and reflex modification. Up until last year he had been visited monthly by an Integrations Officer for evaluation. He was considered a success and visitations would occur once a year by recommendation from the Eval Officer. Theoris was floored. She read more and more.

Akila had a hard time keeping up with Theoris' reading pace. She figured what she did miss Theoris would fill her in or would allow her to read later. Then Theoris stopped on a page titled PSYCHE EVAL. Honute was rated high and potentially powerful. The report also stated that his ability was innate and inert.

Theoris said, "This is good and bad news."

Akila nodded.

"Do you have the baseline test results?" Theoris asked.

Akila nodded. "They're in my Inbox under the directory Subject Honute."

Theoris went back to the Inbox, find the directory, and opened all results pertaining to Honute. "Grab a sit Akila. This might take a while."

"Yes, Doctor." She said while grabbing a chair from the other side of the desk. "What about Honute? He's waiting in your office."

Theoris pressed her lips together. "We'll look at this for a few more minutes. Okay?"

Akila nodded and sat down. She hoped Honute had a limitless well of patience. Who knew when Dr. Theoris would be satisfied enough to act. Suddenly, Akila was afraid of Honute. She was right, he was definitely a dichotomy. He was one that could kill them both and probably not lose any sleep afterwards. She hoped that her feelings about him being kind, gentle, and caring were correct. Akila wondered when the last time Honute got angry who got killed. Then she shuddered. Was he super violent and was that the reason Hypatia was divorcing him? Life got complicated and she didn't like that.

Honute sat on the couch and sipped tea. He thought over events that happened during the last several days. He viewed this bit of time as an introspection of his life thus far. There were several things that were established. Hypatia left him, he was in love with Akila, and he would be physically changed - which was what he was being told. Whether any or all three things happening were a good or bad thing was a point of view. Today, it was a good thing. Tomorrow? He shrugged and sipped again.

Several moments passed and he sipped the tea again. It was cold and the bark taste bit harshly. He had been waiting for the last hour and Dr. Theoris and Akila hadn't returned. He got up and stretched his body. Since he started this whole magick stuff he stopped his morning exercise routine. In the mornings he would wake up about two hours before Hypatia and go through a whole series of body dynamic stress positions. He actually liked the fact that his body stayed rock solid, even after years of being away from the Royal Army. While his fellow priests expanded their waist line and got heavier, he stayed trim and fit. But today he felt bloated and lethargic.

He stepped to the middle of the floor, tied the bottom of his robe in a knot and slipped out of his tunic. Then he stood on his tip toes, and stretched the palms of his hands to the floor. He locked his knees and bent at the waist. Then, with his palms flat and solidly on the floor he lifted his legs and straightened out his hip. The bottom of his robe bunched down to his waist. He ignored it.

Honute pointed his toes to the ceiling. He stiffened his back, arms and legs. He took in a deep breath and lifted himself up on his finger tips. Then he lifted one hand away and made a loose fist with the other. He concentrated to hold his balance with the remaining hand. Only his thumb, index, and middle finger held him up. He relaxed his mind and imagined himself as a straight metal pole. His personal best was one hour twelve minutes.

Akila and Theoris stood at the doorway mesmerized as they watched Honute handstand on only three fingers. After several seconds, Theoris coughed lightly.

Honute looked up, smiled, and slowly brought his feet down. He straightened out and untied the bottom of his robe and placed his tunic back on. He shrugged and said, "I didn't know how long it would be, so I started occupying my time."

Theoris nodded. "I see. I would have never imagined priest training to be so rigorous."

Honute blushed. "It's not. That was from another period in my life. The only good thing about it was that it got me into peak physical conditioning."

Theoris looked him up and down. Akila did the same. Both remained silent for a moment. Theoris cleared her throat. "Well, Honute, please have a seat."

Honute sat back on the couch and waited.

Akila elected to stand at the doorway.

Theoris tapped on the keyboard and watched the monitor. "Your test results are in."

Several moments ticked by.

Honute leaned forward, "Yes?"

Theoris sat back. "Honute, please forgive my sometimes clinical demeanor. I occasionally get caught up in the moment. The truth is, I could not have asked for a better subject."

Honute said, "That is good news then?"

Theoris nodded, "Yes and no."

"Pardon?" Honute said.

"Well, it's good in the way that we'll get near maximum yield in our testing. It's bad, because you are not a good representative of the rest of the Blessed Lands."

Honute just said, "Oh."

Theoris nodded and continued. "You're in the small percentile group of zero point zero one. That's about one in nine thousand.

Honute nodded. "Sounds more bad than good."

Theoris forced a smile. "We'll manage well enough." She leaned back into the chair trying to look and feel comfortable. Her stomach ached and her head spun slightly. It felt like her mind raced to catch up with itself. She cleared her throat and said. "Well, Honute, how are you feeling?"

"I'm doing okay. Nothing much to complain about." He smiled and Theoris recognized the smile, with added character lines, as the one in the photo. "I'm sensing that this day has been a bit taxing on you. Am I correct?"

Akila felt a chill run down her back.

Theoris slowly nodded. "Yes, but not to worry. We will move forward in the research. Tomorrow begins the trials. We'll start off with a small dose and begin testing."

Honute nodded.

Theoris looked at her timepiece. It was nearly six pm and she had a date with Hypatia. The pain in her stomach increased and see broke out into a light sweat. She looked over to Akila and said. "Akila, I won't be able to take Honute home today, would you mind using one of the University vehicles to take him?"

Akila nearly froze. "Sure, Dr. Theoris." Then added, "May I use the department gas card? You know the tanks in those things are never full."

Theoris nodded and reached into her drawer. She pulled out the gas card along with a debit card. "Here, you two have a nice dinner on me. The limit is set to 500 per day.." She tried to make her smile look natural.

Akila reached out and took both cards. "We will." She intended to get fat tonight and maybe drunk. She hoped Honute liked beef and spirits.

Honute nodded in agreement. "Thank you for your kindness Theoris. May Isis watch over you tonight." He bowed slightly.

Chapter 15

It was past seven when Akila and Honute walked into the Marble Greek. Akila favored this restaurant because of the feel and atmosphere. She liked the idea of the many marbled statues that dotted the wall. It gave the area an off-beat look that was clearly and most decidedly not Egyptian. She remembered reading about the Greeks in High School and became fascinated and caught up with their love of art and sculptures. She particularly enjoyed looking at the statues, as they seemed life-like. She could swear on occasion that a statue would move. There! Just a second ago, she thought she saw the chest of one statue rise. It was of a tall slender female. Her features were exotic and foreign but very captivating and, if a bit different, pleasing to the eye. The thing that most attracted Akila's eye to the sculpture was the gliding and sensual body lines. The female was leaning against the wall with one shoulder lifted slightly away from the wall. She looked at Honute who was seated across from her. He seemed to be relaxed but she couldn't tell. He sipped at his glass of wine, which moved him back up a niche or two on her scale. She kicked herself for being afraid of him earlier. He really was a nice guy. So what if the report said he was a soldier. He had been successfully integrated back into society. Wasn't that the important part? It didn't matter his previous life, just his current one. She looked into his eyes and thought it would be nice to wake up to them. He was a great listener. She supposed that's what made him good at being a priest. So, there should be nothing wrong, except she had this small nagging doubt about Honute's demeanor being his own or one planted in him. She had read a little on re-integration. Its many different forms of changing and reshaping human behavior were a triumph to social science. All soldiers were expected to receive some form of the treatment. He looked back and sipped at the vino and made a comment about the statues seeming so life-like and if he stared at one long enough he swore it moved. Akila smiled and sipped at her own glass. The alcohol had already gone to her head and the outside of her cheeks felt warm and numb at the same time. The Host, Alexano, brought another bottle of wine, popped the cork. He filled both glasses to the rim and left the bottle on the table.

Honute took a good swallow and smiled.

Akila smiled back and took a sizable swig herself. "Honute, why the priesthood?" There! As soon as she said it she felt better. She had agonized over how she would breech the subject, but the alcohol made it easier. She reasoned she could always blame everything on the booze.

Honute filled his glass with wine. He lifted the glass up to his face, swirling the contents he gazed through the red liquid. Akila's face shimmered within the wine. She was pretty he thought. Then a twinge of guilt hit him. Here he was enjoying the company of a brilliant, beautiful, sexy, and younger woman. He tried to push the guilty feeling aside but like a small sore it bit at his heart. He wondered what Hypatia was doing at the moment and wished he hadn't wondered. There was no particular reason why he shouldn't enjoy himself. He had worked long, hard, and many hours at the temple. This diversion was most welcomed. Thoth had been watching over him, he decided, and made it possible to feel happy again. He swirled the glass expertly and the wine seemed to part down the center showing a better, less transparent, image of Akila. Yes, she was most beautiful. 'How far will it go?' Honute thought.

Akila felt a chill. She couldn't tell if it was from the draft that just blew in – The host opened the door and a gust of wind entered, or if it was her reaction to Honute's gesture.

Honute took a drink. "It seemed like the right thing to do at the time. I suppose it is a way to pay for my actions in the war, a sort of penance. As a priest I can help people, give them hope. In the past . . . "He paused for a moment and chose his words carefully. ". . . I took hope away."

Akila swallowed hard and took a drink. She tried not to make it seem she needed the drink badly. Her smile was casual, as if she understood and supported him; she tried to make it look natural. Deep inside down through to her soul she wondered.

Hypatia and Theoris lay in bed. Their lovemaking abruptly interrupted by Theoris' sudden stomach pain. Hypatia had climaxed earlier and was taking her time to bring Theoris to one. She had been teasing Theoris with her tongue and had just wrapped her arms around her thighs when Theoris' stomach knotted up in a bunch of hard twitches. Hypatia thought it was her doing but then realized the spasms were not from an orgasm. She released her hold on Theoris' legs, moved up beside her and took Theoris' head in her arms.

Theoris bit back a scream. Wave after wave of painful convulsion racked her body.

Hypatia, worried, asked, "Should I call a doctor?"

Theoris squeezed her eyes tight. A second later the pain disappeared. She shook her head. "No, I'm all right. The pain is gone and I'm feeling better."

Still worried, Hypatia looked into her lover's eyes. There was something Theoris wasn't telling. It wasn't as if Theoris owed her information. This was their second night of lovemaking, which hardly made a relationship. Hypatia decided not to ask and would let Theoris speak her mind when she was ready. "Can I get you anything?"

"Yeah, a bottle of Honey Ale," Theoris said.

Hypatia replied, "Honey Ale? Is it your stomach that is bothering you?"

Theoris smiled at the younger woman and nodded, "But not from physical problems. I need to relax and the Ale would be the best choice at this moment."

Hypatia nodded and left to retrieve the bottle. She would bring the entire star-pack. They might as well drink together.

It was dark and for a brief moment Akila was filled with terror. She was in a strange bed, in a strange place. A strange body lay next to her. Then she remembered she was in Honute's bed and the body was a sleeping Honute. He had his arm wrapped around her and softly snored in her ear. She untangled herself and softly slipped from the bed and walked, bumped her way to the bathroom. She closed the door and flipped at the light switch. The fluorescent bulb flicked on with a bright flash. She shielded her eyes and rapidly blinked them. They stung and burned and watered. She squeezed her lids shut tight until the hurting went away and slowly opened them again. Her hangover filled her head, pushing outward. She opened the medicine cabinet and saw all sorts of bottles. She was looking for a pain-killer. On the third shelf, she found it. It was for stomach-cramps. Akila took two tablets and scooped a handful of facet water into her mouth. She wouldn't be on her period for another three weeks but she knew the tablets would work just as well on a headache. She closed the cabinet door and stared into the mirror. Her hair was messed up and she had bags under her eyes. She looked around for a comb and noticed several on the counter. Then it hit her. This was Hypatia's bathroom. She slowly picked up a comb and pulled loose hair from its teeth. Those she tossed in the waste basket. She had a nag of guilt as she combed her hair using another woman's comb. Then the guilt slipped away and was replaced by perverse triumph. A smile formed on her face as she realized she made love to a married man, an ex-soldier and a priest. She suddenly became giddy and her nipples stiffened with excitement. She thought back to how it happened and breathed a sigh of relief. Honute was a wonderful lover. She came three times in thirty minutes. His powerful arms twisted and lifted her into positions regular men wouldn't be able to hold for long. He finished her off in a mind-numbing blur of rapid thrusts that had her clawing at his back and the sheets. She remembered she screamed once, but that was from the second orgasm. The third had her mind spiraling into ecstasy. Time seemed to stop and speed up in spurts. She remembered the fourth and fifth orgasm had her limply fumbling at the air and grabbing nothing. After that she remembered nothing. Then she woke up, terrified. It was a new experience for her – being in the bed of a married man that frightened and intrigued her at the same time. The few men she had had in the past were but mere boys compared to Honute. They would meekly hump her backside, breathing hard, thinking they were all that, only to irritate her more than amuse her. Akila's last lover was a med student in his last year of didactic training. He was tall, dark and dazzlingly handsome. He had a big dick and a long tongue. Problem was half the time he couldn't get it up and when he did it was mostly semi-hard. One day he walked in holding a strap-on dildo and asked her to wear it. She did, intrigued to see his reaction. He stood back and eyed her. He got stiff as a board and asked her to enter him. She slipped in easily and he nearly exploded. He yelled out how much it felt good and for her to do it harder. She complied but decided that would be the last time. Moments later he screamed and came hard enough to shot the length of the bedroom. After that she made excuses. He eventually got the hint, packed up the tool, and went to intern about a thousand miles away. She had hopes for him in the beginning. That was then. She looked back into the mirror and smiled. Her hair was very nearly neat and smooth. She found tooth paste and finger brushed her teeth. Then she grabbed a wash cloth and cleaned herself. She walked back into the bedroom and climbed on top of her sleeping lover. She kissed him on the back of his neck and rubbed herself on him. When he responded she nibbled on his ear.

Honute rolled over and took Akila in his arms. He kissed at her neck and ran his tongue along her jaw line. He smiled and was stiff again. He moved her hand to caress it.

Akila slipped the covers off him and ran her hand down his stomach to his legs. Honute gently coached her hand into grabbing his stiff self. She took it and stroked gently. He arched his back and let out a small moan. He moved his fingers between her legs and found the soft silky tuff of hair. His index finger found her clitoris and he swirled his finger around and on top of it. Akila moaned and breathed heavily. When she was wet he slipped the finger in and rubbed the inside. She released him and grabbed his jaw and kissed his passionately. She slipped her tongue in his mouth and worked it as hard as she could.

Honute rolled onto his back and lifted Akila gently up on top of him. He settled her down slipping inside. Then he worked his hips up and down until she let out a scream and asked him to stop. He laughed and softly said, "No." He wasn't ready yet.

Thirty minutes later a limp Akila lay next to Honute. Her thighs sporadically trembled uncontrollably. She smiled and moaned and caressed Honute. Moments later both were asleep again. Off to a peaceful and wonderful slumber land of beautiful sounds and tastes – just like their love making.

Chapter 16

Thank Thoth the laws permitted him some leeway, thank Isis the law permitted Akila some leeway! He would have been branded and she would have been stoned.

Honute sat on the examination table waiting for one of the doctors to enter. He waited, dressed in a hospital gown recounting last night's event. Akila woke him up from a frightful dream. In it he saw Hypatia screaming and yelling at him. She was mad and hurled painful words at him. Then she had a gun and fired. He woke up to Akila kissing his neck. All was better with the Blessed Lands and he felt that Thoth was smiling down on him. Thoth had to be rewarding him for some unknown deed he was about to do. Honute realized his smile was not forced for the first time in many months. He was happy and though he had not known Akila for very long he hoped she was happy as well.

Theoris stepped into the room first. Akila was several steps behind her. Theoris walked over to a monitoring system in the corner. It read Honute's pulse, temperature and blood pressure. Occasionally, a power led would flicker on and off and a low tone hummed as background noise. She turned to say something and saw that Akila was leaning against the exam table. One thigh was resting lightly on the edge of the table and she was teasing her hair. Akila was wearing a loose version of her usual dress wrap – Greek influence, which allowed the leg to rest comfortably on the table. Both were softly talking. "Akila?"

Akila looked up. She seemed to be glowing. "Yes, Doctor?"

Theoris frowned. "I'm sorry." She smiled. "I forgot what I was going to ask."

Akila and Honute laughed.

Theoris looked toward the door and said, "I'll be back in maybe thirty minutes. If Dr. Rivota arrives before I return have her proceed without me."

Akila nodded. "Yes, Doctor."

Theoris quickly walked out the room, down the hall, down the stairs. She stepped out into the open area and hastily walked toward Hypatia's building. She took the stairs and nearly ran down the hall to Hypatia's office. She stopped just in front of the doorway to catch her breath. After a moment she lightly rapped on the door frame.

Hypatia was studying notes from one of the associate professors. The writing was a squiggle of jumbled mangled script. She had been looking at one paragraph for the fifth time when she heard a light tapping at her door. She placed the papers down and walked over to the door. She opened it and saw Theoris grinning ear to ear.

Theoris stepped in happy as a lark. Her smile was wide and she felt light on her feet. Hypatia had opted to wear a tan dress wrap with a traditional emerald necklace. It clung to her body and gave her a sexy look. Theoris closed the door behind her and grabbed Hypatia by the jaw. She kissed her passionately and crushed Hypatia close to her body. The emerald pressed firmly against her chest and made a small niche just below the collarbone.

After several seconds, Hypatia pulled away. "I missed you too!"

Theoris cupped one of Hypatia's breasts and whispered in her eye. "Tonight, you are mine."

Hypatia said, "Oh really? How's the stomach?"

Theoris replied, "Much better. It was definitely a mental thing. I really do feel much better."

Hypatia smiled, "Okay, so what mental thing that happened between then and now made you better."

Theoris opened her mouth to say what she thought was happening between Honute and her assistant, but it occurred to her that Hypatia might not be happy. What to do, what to do? She could tell the truth and hope Hypatia would find the irony in the situation. She pursed her lips together and said, "Ferruk inserted himself into the project."

Hypatia stiffened. "Oh? Really?"

Theoris nodded, "Well, Ferruk, did some posturing and Honute meekly bowed down to him. It was pathetic." She made an ugly face. In that part she wasn't lying. It had been a pathetic scene to her. "Well, afterwards, I think it put Akila off. She'll be working with Honute closely and things will go better if they have a decent understanding. They seemed to be getting along, now."

Hypatia slowly said, "And that was the thing that got you all knotted up inside?" It sounded a bit silly. A grown woman – in charge of tens of millions of dollars of equipment and grants, who has made men tremble and cry, worry about how her assistant likes her husband.

Theoris nodded. "Silly, I know, that was just the last of a bad day and I think I was too focused on it." That last spin may have saved her lie.

Hypatia nodded.

Theoris said, "Ferruk, I feel is going to be a real pain in the ass. Having my inner circle world function well will help me deal with him." She took a deep breath.

Hypatia thought for a second and then laughed.

Theoris, confused, laughed too, but not as hard. "What?"

Hypatia kissed her on the cheek. "You are human. At first I thought you were trying to cover something up."

Theoris' laugh was forced but sounded natural. "Cover something up?"

"Yes," Hypatia said, "like, you or your assistant falling in love with Honute."

The laugh wasn't forced this time.

"But since your ex-husband is involved I can understand all the stress." Hypatia thought a moment. "I'm glad, Akila? That's her name?"

Theoris nodded.

"I'm glad Akila can work with Honute. He really is a very sweet man, and most women would just love him. If Akila winds up liking him that's okay, she can have him. Any woman can have him, I don't care. I've made up my mind. Besides, I had been feeling a little guilty about us."

Theoris was surprised, "Really?"

Hypatia grinned, "Yeah. I hadn't made love to him in several weeks and here I am having sex. I doubt Honute would have had a chance to find someone. He can be so humble and passive at times. He would be working too hard not to hurt everyone's feelings to be aggressive."

Theoris thought about that remark for a moment. Something was adding up. "Would it trouble you if I ask you questions about him later tonight?"

Hypatia frowned, "What do you mean? Trouble me?"

"Well, I think I'm going to need to do a personality profile on him. I was able to access his old military bio and a few questions came to mind."

"Well, I suppose so, if you only have a few questions? I really don't want to talk about him all that much. I'd like to plan my next step and move on with my life. I know it's not your fault that by a strange twist of fate he winds up being part of the research of my lover."

Theoris heard mixed messages, but she had some satisfaction that Hypatia referred to her as lover. "I promise I'll keep it short. Would you like anything special tonight? My treat."

Hypatia stepped up close to Theoris. "Well, I had wanted to try that Greek restaurant near here."

Theoris said, "The Greek Marble?"

"Yes, that's the one. I read in the Daily Papyrus Food Review that the food was great."

Theoris closed the space between the two and pressed her chest up against Hypatia's. She reached around and gave Hypatia's cheek a squeeze. "If food will make you happy then Greek it will be." She pressed her hips firmly against Hypatia's and slowly gyrated. She slipped her leg between Hypatia's and moved it up and down.

"You got time to fool around?"

Hypatia responded in like and hugged Theoris tightly. She pressed her lips against Theoris' and slipped her tongue in. The kiss turned passionate.

Theoris started to lift Hypatia's dress up when there was a knock at the door.

Hypatia cursed softly, said, "One moment, please."

The door knob turned and both women untangled themselves from each other. Dogola, Hypatia's new assistant stepped in.

He looked up from some papers he was reading, startled said, "Oh, I'm sorry Doctor Hypatia. I thought you said, 'Come in, please.' "

Hypatia nearly snatched the papers from his hand but caught herself. "Never mind. Dogola, this is Doctor Theoris. She is Director of the Social Sciences and Behavior department. You see her you jump. She has priority over all phone calls, understand?"

Dogola looked at both women. For a brief moment he felt he interrupted something but pushed it aside. "Yes, Doctor, I understand. Is there anything I can get you?"

Theoris spoke up, "Well, I should be going. I just wanted to give you the news. I'll see you later in the day to discuss that project." No need to start rumors.

Hypatia said, "Yes, thank you." She picked up on the tone. "I am clear after six. I can answer any questions you may have."

Theoris stepped around Dogola and headed back to Akila and Honute. Things were still a bit uncertain, but she felt giddy all the same. One thing she decided she had to know whether or not Akila and Honute were doing more than talking. Odd, she thought, how one could feel some jealousy over the affections given by someone you know and like to someone you don't really know. Tonight would rest two things, hopefully – Honute's past and his present. She looked at her timepiece. Honute should be ready to receive his first injection. She hurried out the building. This she, decided, was something she wanted to see.

Honute was relaxed and meditating. An IV line ran from a plastic bag, hung upside down from a metal pole, to the antecubetal area of his arm. Akila was sitting in front of the monitoring station. She had a notepad in her hand and was writing something. Theoris presumed it to be data from the monitoring instruments.

A short rather round middle-aged woman in a white lab coat leaned over Honute. She had the flat end of a stethoscope pressed to Honute chest. Theoris watched Dr. Rivota with a careful eye. She liked the woman on a professional level; however, Rivota was known to be a gossiper. "Priest Honute, please take a deep breathe."

Honute inhaled deeply. It went on for a full ten seconds.

Rivota said, "Let it out slowly. Okay, another deep breath but not as long . . . thanks, and let it out slowly." She palpated his chest with two fingers. Then she called out. "Akila, what is Priest Honute's BP?"

Akila looked up from writing. "110/65."

"And Pulse rate?"

"Fifty-two."

Rivota stood back. "Well, Priest Honute . . ."

"Just Honute, please." Honute said.

Rivota continued. "You are in outstanding physical conditioning. Most adolescents wished they had health like yours."

Theoris stepped up and looked at the IV.

Rivota said, "You missed the action about ten minutes ago. Honute is a good patient."

He smiled.

Akila glanced his way and smiled broadly.

Theoris caught the smile. So did Dr. Rivota.

Rivota patted him on the thigh and said, "Well, Honute, I'll send in one of my assistants to help with the monitoring. We're going to leave you on the IV for another four hours. Tell us if you feel strange or different, okay?"

Honute nodded.

Rivota walked toward Theoris. Both stepped outside the room. "Where'd you find this one?" Rivota asked. "He is in outstanding shape and what eye candy."

Theoris blinked several times.

Rivota said, "I'd love to find him under my sheets." She looked at Theoris. "Tell me, Theoris, I know you would have liked to taste him."

"What do you mean 'would have liked to?'" Theoris replied.

Rivota smiled broadly. "Akila, your assistant, is having sex with him." She laughed.

Theoris knew it. It was that obvious. And if Rivota could tell after seeing a chance look then what would Hypatia see? Theoris smiled back. "Really? You really think they are having sex?"

Rivota grinned, "And how! I could practically smell the pheromones in the air." She looked back into the room and whispered, "I'd suck his dick."

Theoris was mortified.

Rivota laughed. "Well, wouldn't you, if he offered it?"

"I can't believe we are having this conversation?"

"Oh, come now, I know you haven't been totally off men. They do have their uses."

Theoris stood staring in stunned silence.

Rivota said, "Well, I'm feeling pretty aroused by the thought. I think I'll break for lunch early and have one of my interns occupy my time."

Theoris stared wide-eye at her, horrified that Rivota so much as admitted to having some sort of relationship with one of her interns. The rumors had been true. She hadn't believed it. She asked, "How long?"

Rivota smiled. She got Theoris' attention. "With this particular one? Maybe a few months. Some of the other department heads have been doing it longer."

"W-What?"

"You've had to have known, Theoris."

Theoris shook her head.

"Well, you do now. Meet me for lunch tomorrow and I can give you the run down. You'd be very surprised."

Theoris nodded her head as she watched Rivota quickly fade down the hallway. She turned and wondered what Rivota meant by 'You'd be very surprised.' Did she know something? Theoris shuddered and swallowed hard. And did Rivota know about her and Hypatia? Damn this was getting complicated. Why couldn't she have just left Hypatia alone? An upset Honute might be survivable – his conditioning was something to consider. He seemed to be genuinely docile. Hypatia was something entirely different. Theoris heard about her temper on more than one occasion. It wasn't that it was violent and sudden. Rumor had it that it was slow to burn but the heat was always on. Then one day, boom! An upset Hypatia boded bad news.

Chapter 17

Ferruk sat at the desk in the VIP suite of Hotel New Heliopolis. He looked at some papers on his desk and shifted them to the side. A copy of a newspaper clipping was in front of him. Earlier, he made a request to the local library to find as much data as they could on the Oracle. Knowing the Oracle came from the Heliopolis region made the chance of finding unique bits of information the more likely. The librarians of New Heliopolis Repository and Library jumped through hoops to help him. He chuckled when one of them dropped to his knees and swore on his Mother's life that he would do the best that he could to assist the Great Priest Ferruk. One of the body guards retrieved the copy and now it lay in front of him. Ferruk mused over the article. It was about a young boy who miraculously survived a dilapidating and almost always terminal disease. The young boy was age six and the newspaper explained that a local Oracle had treated the young man. The treatment was very dangerous and sometimes worse than the disease. The young man survived and Pharaoh heard about the cure and ordered the local town Oracle to have an audience with him. She did and later became the Royal Oracle. The same Oracle Ferruk had been receiving those confounded and sometimes misleading predictions of hers. Then he caught a familiar name within the article. The young boy's name was Honute.

He began to think of all the time the Oracle feed him information. She gave him little tidbits here, small tiny morsels there. She manipulated him. He didn't know whether to be enraged with her for all the years she maneuvered him, or at himself for not seeing it sooner. He sat there thinking what to do. He felt that as long as she was the right ear of Pharaoh he could never have true power. He had to get rid of her, finally. He turned to his most trusted bodyguard, Ivoniyut, and hatched a plan. During the Cursed Wars Ivoniyut had been a sniper for Pharaoh. Ferruk thought his talent a curiosity at first but gained significant appreciation for his particular talent. Today, Ivoniyut would have a new assignment. "Ayruyi, come here, please."

Ayruyi stepped out of the kitchen. She had been preparing her master's lunch. She walked over to him fearing the worst. She stopped in front of him and dropped to her knees. She reached out to lift his robe up when he stopped her.

He chuckled to himself that she had read his mind so perfectly. "Not now, I have something more important I want you to do. I'm going to send you on a special mission for me."

Ayruyi, perplexed, looked up. "Yes, Master?"

Ferruk smiled. "It's something that will suit your wonderful talents." He laughed at her confused look. "After lunch, summon your Father here, I'm going to be without your services for a few days." Then he lifted his robe up and smiled. "For the moment you can attend me. Be quick, I want to eat lunch and make it on time to a meeting in an hour."

Honute had been thinking about Akila when he felt something. It came on him fast. It was like a burst of heat that swept through his body. He was thinking about the night before and remembered the cold air biting his skin. He and Akila had just finished making love and they both laid there sweaty and exhausted. A draft had whooshed in from an open window. It felt frigid but welcomed. He had wanted to grab a blanket to warm up but the feel of Akila smooth skin against his was too pleasing. Then he thought about the blanket and he suddenly became hot.

Akila jumped when the monitors beeped loudly. The graphs and recorders wiggled and flashed excitedly. For a moment she was frozen with surprise. Then she leapt into action. She grabbed the clipboard and started checking things. She looked over to Honute who seemed to be sweating. She ran over. "Are you okay? How are you feeling?"

Honute wiped sweat from his brow. "Warm. No, I feel hot." He started breathing rapidly and got light headed. The room began spinning and he reached out to Akila to steady himself. "I feel dizzy."

Delenoah, one of Rivota's assistant stepped into the room. He had a clipboard in his hand and nearly dropped it when Akila startled him.

Akila heard a sound at the door and saw Delenoah stepping through. She yelled, "Get Dr. Rivota! STAT!"

Delenoah stood there for a moment. He heard the alarms and saw Honute, drenched in sweat and breathing rapidly. He snapped out of it and ran.

Honute started shaking uncontrollably.

One of the monitors exploded, sparked and fizzled. The alarms seemed to get louder as another monitor sparked loudly.

Rivota ran with several nurses and another medical doctor behind her. Theoris came in last.

Honute's eyes slipped upward into his head and he started thrashing against the bed.

Akila grabbed at his arms but the sweat made them slippery.

Rivota reached his side and grabbed him. The others each grabbed a limb and pressed them firmly into the mattress. Rivota grabbed Honute's head to steady it. She noted the eyes and yelled "OxyNeutripin! Three cc's!"

A nurse disappeared.

Theoris stood helpless as the chaotic scene unfolded before her eyes.

A monitor exploded and electricity arced madly across the walls and ceiling.

The nurse returned and slipped the needle end of the syringe into a slot along the IV line. He pressed the plunger down and pale blue liquid snaked its way through the clear plastic line.

Honute thrashed harder and flung a nurse against a wall.

Rivota yelled, "Keep him steady!" She looked around and saw

Theoris standing alone. "Get some ice and place it in a bag. Quick!"

Theoris moved a leg. It seemed that her feet had been glued to the floor. Then she moved the other leg. It was easier. Then the first again, then the second. Then she ran to the refrigerator, opened it, and grabbed several trays of ice. She found a plastic pouch and threw the ice in it. She ran back.

Akila had literally tossed herself on top of Honute. He was burning up and it felt like her skin was blistering.

Theoris ran up to Honute and placed the bag of ice on his forehead. Within seconds it was a bag of warm water and leaking all over the place.

The overhead sprinklers burst and rained water on everything.

Two more people entered the room and grabbed Honute.

Then suddenly he stopped and all the alarms went silent.

The sprinklers continued for a second then stopped.

Then the EKG monitor alarm went off. The continuous audible tone filled the room.

Rivota pushed Akila off Honute and felt for a pulse along the carotid artery. Nothing. She tilted his head back with the palm on her right hand and used her left hand to open his lower jaw. She pressed her thumb firmly against chin and the jaw opened. She placed her ear and cheek next to his mouth and waited. Nothing. She looked at Theoris and said. "Get an AED and bring it back."

Theoris ran out the room.

Rivota pinched Honute's nose closed with the hand that rested on his forehead and gave two quick and deep breathes. She released his nose and hovered her cheek above his face. She didn't feel a thing. "Begin chest compression."

The nurse placed one hand, palm down, over the other and positioned them over Honute's chest. She had felt for the Xiphod tip to make sure she would not be pressing down on it. She locked elbows and shoulder and pumped up and down from the waist. "One and two and three and four and . . ." She said out loud to a count of five. She stopped.

Rivota pinched Honute's nose and breathed in two good breaths. She watched his chest rise and fall with each breath. She stopped.

The nurse did another five pumps and Rivota had finished the second breath when Theoris ran in. She yelled, "The AED is here."

Theoris worked quickly. She removed the wired chest pads from the plastic bag and plugged one end into a socket on the device. She hit the "on" button.

The machine beeped and a voice, from the machine, said, "Please place pads on chest."

Theoris removed the backing from the pads. She dried a large spot on his chest and placed one pad over his right breast and the other down over his left side.

The device beeped and said, "Analyzing. Please do not touch the patient." It beeped again. "Analyzing. Please do not touch the patient."

Akila held her breath while she watched helplessly.

The device beeped again. "Shock treatment advised. Charging. Please stay away from the patient."

Theoris looked around and said out loud. "Clear! I am clear."

Rivota and the nurse both said, "Clear."

The device said. "You may deliver shock now."

Theoris pressed a button marked, "Shock."

Honute's body tensed.

The device said, "Analyzing. Shock advised. Charging."

Theoris and the others went through the routine one more time.

Then the device said, "You may touch the patient and resume BLS."

Rivota placed the side of her cheek near Honute's mouth and nose. She felt air. She placed two fingers near the base of the jaw. She felt a pulse.

Honute opened his eyes. He felt spent.

Rivota asked. "How do you feel?"

Honute lifted himself up. "Like I ran thirty miles."

Rivota nodded. "You gave us a scare."

Honute looked around and noticed everyone in the room. He was wet except for a spot on his chest and side. "What happened?"

Rivota smiled and said, "You died."

Akila had made her way to Honute's side and placed her hand on his thigh.

He looked into her eyes and she nodded, then he fell asleep.

Theoris watched the interaction between Honute and her assistant. A knot hit her in the stomach. No doubt now. Her life just got complicated.

Chapter 18

It was about seven that evening when everything was back in order. Thankfully the data hadn't been destroyed. Theoris was sorting the whole mess when Hypatia walked in. Theoris looked up and smiled. Hypatia was a bright shiny distraction most welcomed now. She felt exhausted though she had done anything she could and to make matters worst Ferruk had walked in after all the chaos. She was drenched in water and looking sad and tired. He looked around the room and asked what happened. It was a blur after that. And now that Honute, with Akila watching, was resting peacefully in one of the private hospital rooms on campus she could take a breather.

Hypatia quietly walked in and sat on the sofa. She heard what happened and had mixed feelings about the whole incident. Her first impulse was to run to Honute's side. In some way she still cared about him and worried. She considered dropping everything and sitting by the hospital bed and waiting until he woke, then she heard that Akila, Dr. Theoris' assistant was occupying that spot. Rumors about the two already circulated through the ranks. She decided to stay away. That decision nagged at her for hours. "You must think I'm the worst kind of bitch." Hypatia said out loud.

Theoris had thought that but said, "No, not really. You've made a decision and you are being firm with it. Why should I fault you for that?"

Hypatia sighed, "Then why do I think I am?"

Theoris placed some papers aside.

Hypatia said, "I want to be by his side, but I don't. I'm mad at him for being a failure, mad at myself for believing he was not, and kicking myself for wondering if he's okay."

Theoris nodded.

Hypatia stared at her feet for a moment then looked up. "Is he really okay?"

Theoris' throat felt dry and itchy. She nodded and forced a smile. "He's fine, Akila is. . ." She stopped when she saw Hypatia's features darkened at the mention of Akila. "Well, anyway, he's fine." She put away the papers and retrieved a data disk from the computer. If there was time tonight she thought she would look at it. "Let's go home. How about we order something in and go to the Greek Marble tomorrow?"

Hypatia nodded.

Theoris got up and said, "I got you some Honey Dew Ice cream."

Hypatia's face brightened up, "Really?"

Theoris nodded, "Yep and a small jar of Royal honey."

Both women walked out.

Akila was sitting next to Honute's bed when he woke up.

He turned his head over to her and smiled, "How long?"

Akila smiled back and rested her hand on his, "Only a few hours. You remember what happened?"

He shook his head. "Not really. Only that I suddenly got hot and I had a dream about meeting Thoth."

"Really?" Akila said.

Honute nodded. "It was very real. He told me that I had some things to do and that I would need you by my side."

Akila blushed.

Honute clasped his fingers in hers. "He is right. I am glad you are here."

She looked into his eyes and kissed him on the forehead. "So am I."

Ayruyi had been standing in the doorway for several minutes. Anger festered deep in her core as she watched the touching scene between Honute and Akila. She cursed her Father, Pharaoh, and

Ferruk and wished them all dead. She cursed herself as well and began to cry. Sudden grief overwhelmed her.

Akila and Honute heard someone at the doorway.

"Ayruyi, " Honute said, "why are you crying?"

She rushed up to Honute and pushed Akila's hand off his. She grabbed it and placed his fingers on her forehead in a symbolic gesture of submission.

Akila watched with disgust and was about to reclaim Honute's hand when Ayruyi let go, faced Akila, and bowed deeply. "Forgive my personage Akila. I did not mean to offend. My Master Ferruk has sent me on a mission."

Akila blinked several times.

"I see you two and I could only wish I had as you two now have. Forgive my impure thoughts."

Akila frowned. "I don't understand."

"My master had asked me to attend to Priest Honute's needs and appetite, but I would do it without his orders."

Akila asked, "Needs and appetites?"

Ayruyi looked down. "Sex, Personage. I am to be his personal slave for the week. I am to do what Priest Honute commands of me, without question, or my master would have me punished."

Akila shook her head. "This is the modern world. Slaves have rights. He just can't do that."

"Personage, he is High Priest and Vizier of the Middle Regions. Only Pharaoh, the Royal family and a handful of others can command him. Everyone else is but under him. If he says I am Priest Honute's slave for a week I am his slave."

Akila turned to Honute and said, "Honute, you can't let him do that. This is not right."

Honute nodded slowly. A grave expression form on his face. "Akila, I agree, but if High Priest Ferruk instructs it so then it is to be. I . . ."

Ayruyi interrupted. "Personage, I am in love with Honute."

Honute stopped and looked shocked. He turned to Ayruyi and stared deep into her eyes. Honute would have known if she lied.

He had the gift with people.

Akila never once exhaled. She held her breath for what felt like minutes. Ayruyi, slave, to Priest Ferruk, declared her love. Akila didn't know what to say. She was dumbstruck.

Honute touched Ayruyi on the shoulder and said, "Would you forsake me for not being able to return your love?"

Ayruyi turned and stared at her feet. "I only know what is in my heart."

"And I know what is in mine. Would you forsake me?"

Ayruyi looked up, tears in her eyes. "No."

Honute removed the covers and swung his feet over the edge of the bed. "Then we must all leave. I must take you back to Ferruk."

Ayruyi stood still.

Honute stepped forward to the closet to retrieve his robe. He stopped and turned to see Ayruyi's face become pale.

"What's the matter, Ayruyi, surely, Ferruk will understand."

She shook her head. "He would not. He would be angry with me." She collapsed to her knees.

Honute, with robe folded on his arm, caught Ayruyi. He lifted her up and placed her in the bed. He looked at his hand and made a tight fist. He did the same thing with the other hand and pumped both hands into a fist. The muscles groaned like squeezed and pulled leather straps. He shook himself and placed a hand on Akila's shoulder. "That was weird." He said.

Akila asked, "What? Are you okay?"

Honute frowned, trying to sort the thoughts in his head. "I don't know. I feel different, but the same." He flung his fingers toward the bottom portion of the bed and the covers ruffled. He did it again. Nothing happened.

Akila saw what happened. "What was that?"

Honute shook his head. "I don't know. For some reason I knew the covers would move."

Theoris sat by the fireplace and listened to the burning wood crackle. Her thoughts told her deep and far. She was thinking about Honute and what happened earlier today. Then she thought about Hypatia and her statement about being the worst kind of bitch.

Hypatia was next to her holding a book in one hand and a spoon in the other. She had just licked off a mixture of Honey dew ice cream and Royal Honey. She turned the page. It was a scandalously delicious book of an alternative history romance. It was about a world where Egypt fell into antiquity and a strange land called America dominated the world. She had just finished reading a sex scene and stretched out. She gave Theoris a nudge and nuzzled face in her side. "What's on your mind?"

Theoris' eyes refocused. "Nothing much, really. I'm so close with this that I can feel it."

Hypatia sat up. "Your project and Honute?"

Theoris nodded.

Hypatia was silent for a long time. She wanted to be interested, but she was torn with conflicting emotions. How does one reconcile the feelings of talking to one lover about a past lover? She took another spoonful of ice cream. Her thoughts took her to the first month of Honute's and her marriage. It was heaven she told herself. Honute had just been discharged from the service and entered the School of Religion and Antiquital Studies. Pharaoh was paying for the entire program. Back then she thought it was grand. The school, Honute, the potential. Now, it was plain wishful thinking. "Honute was wonderful when we first married."

Theoris looked at Hypatia, "Pardon?"

Hypatia repeated, "He was wonderful when we first married. We made love five, sometimes six and seven, times a day. He just entered school for the priesthood. I thought he was going to make something of it. All the medals he received from Pharaoh's Royal Guards. He was my war hero and everyone knew him."

Theoris listened with intrigue. She hadn't known what started this, but she listened intently.

Hypatia said, "He was destined to become Vizier. And I would have been his wife. Then he changed. After he finished training he told me that a post had opened up in New Heliopolis. It was a small position, but the head instructor had assured him he would be great in the position. That was many years ago and he is still in that same position, years later! And it pissed me off. My plans had been eroded and washed away with each day he washed his statue of Thoth."

Theoris listened, afraid to say anything. She nodded in the right places to assure Hypatia that she was still attentive.

Hypatia got up and went to the kitchen. She brought back an open bottle of wine. She placed a glass in front of Theoris and poured a healthy amount. She did the same with her glass. "What questions did you want to ask me?"

Theoris looked at Hypatia, "Love, you sure? I know you had a lot of stuff on your mind lately."

Hypatia took a swallow and said, "Might as well get what you can now. In a day or two I won't be feeling guilty and I'll lock up on you."

Theoris made herself comfortable and took a swallow of wine. Hypatia had raided her wine cellar and pulled one of the more drier labels. It was bitter on the tongue but had a smooth aftertaste. "How much do you know of Honute's war past?"

Hypatia took another swallow. "Let's see. He had been wounded a dozen times and was once a prisoner of war . . ."

"A POW?" That surprised Theoris. "I'm sorry, continue."

"No problem. He had been captured and tortured. That was just before the truce. He was in the hospital for several weeks."

"Oh, so after the truce was declared the Maya returned him?"

"No, he escaped. Released all the other prisoners and killed every single soldier there. I heard it was amazing."

Theoris' stomach knotted up and she nearly passed out. Blood drained from her face and she turned pale. Hypatia never noticed. She drained away the last of the wine and poured another drink. "Hypatia, did it ever bother you that Honute's past had been so violent?"

She nodded. "At first it did. I was scared but he was so handsome and fine looking in his uniform. The first time he kissed me was like nothing before. He was like a hungry animal caged up for far too long and suddenly released. We had dated a few times. His twin sister, Honuti, got us together. We were in the same Dorm in college and she said I seemed like a nice girl for her brother. He had this air about him that made you feel safe. He watched everything but paid attention to me. The first time we made love was amazing. It was a bit short though. He hadn't had sex in a year. He came in me after five minutes, but it was so strong and powerful that I came too. He apologized, rested and made love to me the rest of the evening. I guess that was what I liked about him. He wasn't arrogant or boastful. He considered my needs and thought what I had to say was important. He treated me like I was the most important thing he'd ever come across. I guess any woman, or man, would be happy to be with him." She drained the glass and poured another glass. Her face was starting to become numb, but she felt warm all over and despite the heat from the fire her nipples stiffened. She slipped out of her clothes and lay naked next to Theoris.

Theoris watched as Hypatia stripped. She glided her eyes over her exquisitely perfect body and drank in the intoxicating view. Hypatia, she told herself, was mana from heaven. Oh how sin of the flesh skews our thoughts.

"But, I want to be the wife of a Vizier, and Honute is not going to be that."

Theoris thought about Ferruk and his own passion. He made Vizier, but he became a monster in the process. She guessed that some women don't worry about having a soul and leading a peaceful happy life of just living. "Has he ever hit you?"

Hypatia laughed. "By Isis' own eyes no. He never once raised a hand to me. I, however, have hit him with everything and anything throwable. I once was so mad at him that I yanked the microwave from the wall and throw it at him. He took the blow on the chest and let it smash to the ground. He said he would clean up the mess later and walked out. I found him in his prayer room stretching. He was nearly naked and it turned me on to see him like that. He had no bruise on his chest, not one, and he was flexing all his muscles. I walked in, dropped to my knees, pulled him out and sucked him in." She giggled, reached up and pinched Theoris on the nipple.

Theoris sucked in some air and stretched. She reached down and caressed Hypatia's perfect breast. The nipple poked out and was hard. She put her glass down and turned her full attention to pleasing this crazy woman, her lover, Hypatia. Neither woman got much sleep that night.

Honute and Akila didn't sleep all that well. Ayruyi insisted on sleeping in the same room. She curled herself up and slept on the floor. Earlier, Honute and Akila had left her in the living room. They thought she was sleeping. At first she seemed to fret about sleeping. Honute would move and she would jump awake and ask if he needed anything. The tenth time Honute nearly lost his temper. He counted from one hundred to one before he said anything. He counted slowly to himself and made Ayruyi stand in front of him and wait until he was done. After he made it to one he told Ayruyi to go to sleep. If he needed anything he would get it himself. She pouted and seemed to think he was going to hit her. After some reassuring she relaxed. So Honute and Akila left her snoozing on the couch, in front of a warm fire. Ayruyi had fixed a large meal and everyone was stuffed. Honute figured the meal should have been enough to quiet her down. When Honute had discharged himself from the University Hospital he took Akila and Ayruyi shopping. He had visited Lucutus, the store owner, for a few minutes and blessed him and his store. Then he collected lamb, vegetables, wine, bread and a jar of Royal Honey. As a last minute thought he picked up a carton of Honey Dew ice cream and dropped it in the basket. It weighed exactly two pounds. Akila was astonished that Honute was able to walk away without paying a cent. He had explained the reason and she nodded approvingly. Honute smiled.

Ayruyi trailed behind carrying most of the groceries. Honute tried to carry everything, but even Akila insisted on helping out. In the end, Honute and Akila carried one bag and Ayruyi carried the rest. She had threatened she'd die of a heart attack if she didn't prove her worth. She wanted to carry everything. It would be most unfitting for a master priest to carry groceries she said. Akila remarked how interesting it was to note who was master and who was slave. Honute and Ayruyi both blushed. Luckily, the trip from the market was short. All three entered the apartment and Ayruyi cooked the meal. Honute and Akila sat on the couch and chit-chatted about nothing. Ayruyi would often look out the kitchen and throw a dirty look toward the two. When Akila caught her looking, Ayruyi blushed deep red, turned away, and ran into the kitchen. She stayed hidden until the meal had been completed and the table set. After a few minutes of bickering, Honute put his foot down and ordered Ayruyi to take a place at the table. She kept saying that a master priest must not do such things. Honute ignored her and once told her to be quiet and enjoy the privilege of eating at all. That shut her up for the rest of the meal. Honute realized that if he wanted Ayruyi to do something he had to speak at her, with a firm stern voice. He decided he was going to have to change that soon.

Chapter 19

Ferruk rose early. He slept badly and cursed his reasoning for giving Ayruyi to Honute for a week. As far as he was concerned, he should have his dick cut off. "Arrutyi," He yelled, "Breakfast you lazy man. Bring me . . . ."

Arrutyi had stepped in with a tray of fruits and vegetables. A tall glass of pomegranate balanced nicely on the tray. "Yes, Master. Where shall I place it?"

Ferruk shot him a burning gaze. The man anticipated him. Today would be a day of hell for the old man Ferruk thought. "Thank you, Arrutyi." He said slowly. "Place the tray on the table. No. The other one. Toward the end. Thank you, you may leave. No, wait. Move the tray to the other side. The other side I said. Get me a woman. Draw my bath water. I'd do you but I don't want to dirty myself. I told you to move the tray to the other side. That's better. Tea, you forgot the tea. What good are you? What am I to do for a week without decent help? No, no, no! The tray is on the wrong side. Move it now or I shall beat you myself. There, leave it. You can't get anything right, can you? Get out until I need you again. The Tray! Move the tray. I thought I said get out!"

Arrutyi bowed and made a hasty retreat. He knew that Master Ferruk was upset with him. Arrutyi dreaded the coming days. He could see it already. The Master was in a foul mood and only the touch of a woman would pacify him.

Theoris sat staring at the computer screen reading Honute's records. She had been at it for over three hours. The records read like a good book. She got sucked in and hadn't strayed away. She scrolled down to the next page and froze. The title page read, "Re-

conditioning Project." She scrolled to the end page and scanned
the reference and citation section. Eighth line from the bottom she
found her name. She swallowed hard and scrolled back to the
beginning of that section. She read. With each line her heart sank
deeper and deeper. It was true. Honute had been re-conditioned
for "re-integrating back into Blessed society." The program and
techniques used to allow Honute to function well in a normal
society were pioneered by Theoris. She got up from the desk. A
part of her was delighted that it worked. Honute was a shining
example of the techniques. Another part was disgusted. She only
created the techniques as a thesis for her Master's. She knew the
Royal Family had commissioned a study of the possibility of one
day using it. The study led to some trial work in helping some of
the criminally insane and sociopath get to a point were they could
function reasonably well in group interactions. Pharaoh himself
sent her a letter of thanks. As he wrote in the letter more of his
people could reach the afterlife by natural causes instead of violent
and untimely death by the insane. She was touched by it. But after
the study ended over fifteen years ago she hadn't heard anything
come of it. It was like it just dropped off the map. It didn't and
Honute was proof of that. She sighed and stopped reading the
report. It was depressing at its best now. Theoris opened up her
email and went through the myriad of messages. The head of the
physicist department answered her email from last week. The
Magnetic Resonance Recorders were ready for research. She replied
and told Dr. Hytuwian that she, Akila and Honute would be there
later in the afternoon, after lunch. She sent off an email to Hypatia
and told her that they would be with Dr. Hytuwian and his staff
after lunch. As a last minute thought, she called up Dr. Rivota. She
wanted to know if she was still open for lunch. Rivota said yes.
Theoris added to the email to Hypatia that she had a lunch-meeting
with Dr. Rivota and that hopefully she would see her at the
physicist lab later in the afternoon. She sent it and secretly wished
that Hypatia would not show up. But since Hypatia was head of the
overall Astronomy and Physicist department, it was the University's

sick joke of the Grand Unification Theory, she had an obligation to invite her and keep her informed. Theoris sat back and sighed again. She looked at her timepiece. It wasn't even nine o'clock yet.

Honute woke up early. He saw Akila snoozing prettily on the bed. He smiled and kissed her on the forehead. Slowly and carefully he untangled himself from the covers and got out of bed. He surveyed the room but didn't see Ayruyi. He slipped on a light robe and walked out of the room. He closed the door, felt someone behind him, turned and faced Ayruyi.

Ayruyi had woken up very early that morning. She always had. It was an old habit. Ferruk often had to be up by four in the morning to start the beginning day prayer. It was his custom to greet the morning sun with words to the gods. She was glad that Master Honute was up early. "Breakfast is ready, Master."

Honute looked at Ayruyi. "Breakfast? You always fix breakfast this early?

Ayruyi nodded. "Master Priest Ferruk demands it."

Interesting Honute thought. A priest must feed the gods first. "What did you fix?"

Ayruyi smiled for the first time since he met her. "Thin fig cakes, Master. You keep a well stocked store board. I cooked eggs and sliced up some honey dew and cantaloupe."

Honute said, "Ayruyi, about you calling me Master. I would prefer you not. I am not your Master, High Priest Ferruk is."

Ayruyi frowned, "But Master Honute. For the rest of the week you are. Please don't ask me not to serve you. That is my only function in life. . ." She stepped closer to Honute, nearly touching him. ". . . to please and satisfy your every desire and whim. I am yours to command." She lowered her voice to a whisper and placed her hands on his shoulders. "I am here for you, Master Honute. Command me to do anything." She rubbed her hips against his side slowly and cooed.

Honute stepped back and nearly tripped on some furniture. He put his arm up to get some distance between him and Ayruyi. He swallowed hard and said, "Breakfast would be fine, then. You can bring it to the table. Set a place for three."

Ayruyi was at first hurt that Honute shied away from her, but she figured she had some time to let him get comfortable around her. Master Ferruk placed high confidence in her "abilities"; she was not going to fail him. She perked up when Honute asked her to set the table. He was at least going to allow her to serve him. "Three, Master?"

Honute nodded. "Yes. Akila, you and myself."

Ayruyi looked startled, "I, master? I can not!"

Honute recomposed himself. "You will. No backtalk." He turned and walked back into the bedroom. He closed the door, locked it, and started breathing again.

Akila stirred and looked up at Honute. She said lazily, "Good morning."

Honute walked over to and sat on the bed. He looked visibly shaken.

Akila sat up and placed her hand on his shoulder. "Honute, are you okay?"

He said, "I don't know. I'm ashamed and upset all at once."

"Why?"

"High Priest Ferruk's servant." He couldn't bring himself to say the word 'slave.' "I think he's violated Ayruyi's rights."

Akila blinked.

"Ayruyi has, well, approached me as something more than a domestic servant."

Akila smiled and bit Honute on the ear. "I don't blame her."

Honute nearly jumped. "Akila! I am serious."

Akila placed her hand between his legs. "So am I."

Despite his shock he got a hard-on.

"And I think you aren't all that shocked?"

Honute blushed and push her hand away. "Really, this bothers me."

Akila looked at Honute for a moment. "You mean she coming onto you didn't turn you on? The way you came in here I thought it made you horny?"

Honute took in a breath of air. He lowered his heart rate and steadied his breathing. Years of training and practice made it easy. He did get excited and it did make him horny. He remained silent.

Akila smiled and kissed him on the cheek. She hugged him. "My Honute." She said. "It does bother you."

He nodded but remained determined to keep quiet. He was too embarrassed.

"That is what men do with female slaves and vice versa."

Honute blushed again.

"My sweet Honute, she is doing only what she knows what to do. In her way, sex is a way to show that you favor her and that you are not mad or displeased. It's sad, but that's how most slaves know how to do some controlling of their own."

He looked into her eyes. "I would never have thought a high priest would do such a thing. We are to respect and help Blessed citizens, not take advantage."

Akila placed her hand on his cheek. "Honute, I think one of the qualities that has attracted me to you is your willingness to give yourself to your fellow citizen." She kissed him on the lips softly.

He didn't fight it, but kissed her softly back.

"We have breakfast waiting for us."

"How did you know?"

She smiled, got up, and walked to the bathroom. "I watched the whole thing." She closed the door.

Chapter 20

Honute, Akila and Ayruyi walked into the office. Theoris looked up, looked at her time piece. 9:05 am. She nodded at Akila. She looked at Honute and wondered how this humble priest was able to kill an entire camp of enemy soldiers. The conditioning had to have been powerful. "Morning Priest Honute, how are you?"

Honute bowed slightly. "Just plain Honute, please."

Theoris smiled and said, "Okay, 'just plain Honute.'"

After a second, Honute smiled, and then laughed.

Everyone in the room laughed. Ayruyi was a bit annoyed at a joke made at her master's expense. But she smiled. It was witty and she liked Dr. Theoris. She stood up to Master Priest Ferruk where others would have caved in like a mud hut built on stilts in a hurricane.

Theoris tapped at her keyboard. "Today is going to be a full day. After lunch we'll be measuring the bioelectromagnetic field around you Honute. My theory states that we should see measurements off the normal."

Honute nodded, not really knowing what she meant, but he had to be polite.

Theoris continued, "Unfortunately, the equipment was not ready until now. I would have liked to have gotten a reading off you before we did the gene therapy."

Honute nodded again.

"How do you feel? Notice anything strange happening?"

Honute and Akila looked at each other. The stare went for several seconds.

Theoris said, "You did, didn't you?"

Honute hesitated.

Theoris said, "It is imperative that you report any anomalies." She gave Akila a stern look. "Akila, I'm not supposed to be telling you this."

Akila nodded. "Yes, Doctor, I know. It was something that could have been a coincidence."

Theoris, impatient now, said, "Tell me."

Akila took a deep breathe. "Just before we left the hospital. Honute said he had a feeling he could make the bed sheets billow."

Theoris said, "Did he?" She looked at Honute, who shrugged.

Akila nodded. "Something happened. It could have been a draft. And when he tried it again, nothing happened."

Theoris mused. "Interesting. What happened immediately before?"

Akila thought for a second and looked at Honute. His face was calm quiet. She looked at Ayruyi and said, "Honute had found out that Priest Ferruk gave Ayruyi to him for a week."

"What?" Theoris exclaimed "That's — that's absolutely absurd. He can't do that." She turned to Honute. "And you accepted her?"

Honute shrugged, "It's not my place to refuse his gift."

Theoris erupted in a torrent of insults. After a moment she exhausted her vocabulary of bad words and turned to Ayruyi. "How do you feel about this?"

Ayruyi looked at Honute.

He nodded.

Theoris snapped. "I'm asking you, not him."

Ayruyi not quite surprised by Theoris' attitude stared at her. Ayruyi was born a slave. So were her father and mother and their parents and parents' before them. Pharaoh, the embodiment of the gods had enforced it. It was not going away. "I do as I am told." She bowed her head slightly.

"And if you were told to kill yourself, what . . ."

Ayruyi had been through this argument with so many well-wishers and do-gooders. To her, they all seemed dumb. It was those silly questions they asked, like the one Theoris just ask. "I'd kill myself."

Theoris shut up for the moment. She had allowed herself to get derailed. Then she cursed Ferruk for getting under her skin. "Okay, we can skip that train of thought for the moment." She looked toward Honute. "What did you feel when you heard the news?"

Honute thought for a second. "Upset, I believe. I thought I wasn't worthy of this gift."

Theoris, wide-eyed, bit her tongue. She counted to ten, waited, counted to ten again, then said. "Okay, you were upset. Then?"

"Then, for some reason I knew I could make the sheet move. It did, but not the second time. It just seemed to have disappeared."

Theoris nodded to herself. Things were adding up in her head and she wasn't sure she liked the outcome. "Honute, what do you remember of the war?" Theoris watched as rage and distorted madness flashed across his face. It was a split second, and if you hadn't been looking for it you would have missed it. Interesting Theoris thought.

Honute answered, "Not much really. I try not to think about it. I'm not too particularly proud but I suppose I did some good things."

Theoris nodded.

"But now," Honute continued, "being a priest makes me happy. I like helping people."

Theoris nodded again. Classic responses. 'Damn!' she thought. Conditioning is deep. She walked over to her desk and checked her email. She read the reply from Hypatia and pursed her lips together. Hypatia was going to be there. Not good, nor bad, but something would come out of it. She looked up. "Akila, how did you do on progressive hypnosis?"

Akila beamed. "I aced the class. Why?"

"Just a hunch, but I'm going to have you put Honute under."

Honute swallowed hard. "Under?"

Theoris nodded, "Just a light trance. It'll help with the test later this afternoon."

Honute bowed his head slightly. "Okay."

Theoris typed out an email to Ferruk. He had asked earlier

about the progress. She suppose this was as good a time to show him something. Significant or not. She hit the send button and she had just committed herself, of a sort, to a man she hated, didn't trust, and under a silly clause, worked for. She looked up. "How about some tea?"

Ayruyi bowed and started to move.

Theoris held up a hand and firmly said, "While you are in my presence, you will not fetch anything. Do you hear me?"

Ayruyi looked over to Honute.

Theoris gritted her teeth.

Honute nodded and Ayruyi nodded back to Theoris.

Theoris assumed it was some sort of victory. She would definitely play the wildcards when Ferruk arrived. He gave Ayruyi to Honute for a week. Technically, she shouldn't listen to him, but she knew that wasn't going to happen. He had too much a strangle hold on her psyche, and from personal experience he wouldn't let go that readily. She got up and walked toward the door. A thought occurred to her and she stopped in front of Ayruyi. "Sit." She said.

Ayruyi sat without hesitation.

Theoris looked at Akila. "Let's make some tea."

Akila followed Theoris out the door.

Honute, still standing, decided sitting would be a good thing. Tea may be a long time coming. He sat at the edge on the sofa.

Ayruyi coughed. "Master Honute –"

"Just plain Honute, please."

Ayruyi didn't continue. She stared at him.

After several seconds Honute said, "Yes?"

Ayruyi remained tight lipped.

Honute sighed, "Okay, you can call me Master."

Ayruyi smiled, "Master Honute, may I get you something. Dr. Theoris is not here."

Honute almost fell off the edge of the sofa. He wanted to laugh, but the situation didn't seem to warrant it. "No, I'm fine. May I get you anything?"

Ayruyi froze. Master Honute must be playing with her. She was caught in one of those dilemmas about doing what you want to do and doing what is right, which was nothing. "I'm fine, Master Honute."

Honute nodded.

Several minutes of silence ticked by before either of the two said anything.

Honute said, "Are you sure I can't get you anything?"

Ayruyi froze again. The dilemma. "No, I'm fine Master Honute, but do you need anything?"

Honute said, "No, I'm fine too."

Ayruyi nodded.

Silence ticked by again.

When Honute thought he may go mad from the silence, Theoris and Akila walked in. 'Oh thank, Thoth!' Honute thought.

Theoris and Akila walked in, each with a tray. A teapot and two cups sat on the each tray. Theoris and Akila walked over to a small table in the corner and placed the trays on top of it. Theoris handed a cup to Honute, Akila handed one to Ayruyi. The group sat in silence for a moment when Theoris said, "Honute, how do you feel about being a priest?"

Honute sat straight and beamed. His smile was almost frighteningly alarming. "I enjoy it a lot. I get to help people who appreciate the temple and the gods. Over the years, people have been moving away from the temples."

"How does that make you feel?" Theoris asked.

An almost frighteningly disheartening frown appeared on his face. "My heart sinks and it troubles me greatly. Our youth are getting into trouble and our society is heading into the underworld without proper preparation. If I could show the world the power of believing in our gods and having faith in their decisions then I would have accomplished a good thing."

"But, Honute, Pharaoh is the embodiment of the gods." Theoris said.

Honute nodded, "Yes, but he is the embodiment of the gods.

And he can't hear all our cries. Pharaoh has powers to attend to earthly problems. He can't solve problems of the heart and soul. He can't help me find my way out into the light of hope and love when I have fallen and stumbled blindly into despair and depression. The gods can help guide us and keep a path of happiness and blessedness. We just have to open our eyes and hearts to get the message." He took a sip of tea.

Theoris thought for a moment. "Pharaoh can't do that? Help us out of despair and depression?"

Honute slowly nodded. "It was Pharaoh's word that had us fighting the cursed ones."

Theoris nodded. The Maya. She understood. "Do you trust Pharaoh?"

Honute took another sip. "He is the embodiment of the gods for all earthly affairs. That includes the mischievous gods as well."

Theoris smiled. It had been a long time since, 'no' she thought it had never happened, since she had talked to a priest who sounded like he had a brain. Then the nagging thought of his conditioning stepped up. It shouted for her to consider that his answers may not be completely and totally his. But she thought, whom every conditioned him did a marvelous job. She'd take that person out to lunch if she could find him or her. She finished her tea. "Honute, I am surprised."

Honute finished his cup. "Surprised?"

She nodded. "You seem to have a balanced paradigm for a priest and I like that."

Honute bowed his head. "The compliment is most welcomed."

Akila and Ayruyi watched the exchange. Both women, as if communicating mentally, got up and took the tea cups and placed them on the trays. Each woman sat quietly, lost in thought. Akila was thinking how she was falling in love with Honute and with Dr. Theoris' approval the feeling deepened. Ayruyi thought how wonderful it would be to have Honute as her master forever. Earlier she resented him letting the doctor bully both of them, but in the last few minutes he said everything she believed all her life.

And he seemed to value her worth. This would be a master to
have.

Chapter 21

Honute lay on the couch in Theoris' office. Ayruyi had been locked outside. She was miffed, but when Honute told her to explore the University and be back in an hour she didn't protest too much. When he handed her a 100 Durham it disappeared and a smile appeared, seconds later she disappeared.

Theoris had dimmed the lights and asked Akila to hypnotized Honute.

Akila sat in a chair next to Honute. "Honute, please focus your eyes on the spot on the ceiling. Do you see it?"

Honute nodded.

"Take a deep breath, hold it, let it out. Do it again. You feel a tingly sensation on the top of your head. It feels relaxing and the sensation is getting stronger. Tell me what it feels like."

Honute felt the sensation on the top of his head. At first it felt like an itch and he so wanted to scratch it, then it turn pleasant. "It feels nice. Relaxing -"

"I want you to enjoy it spreading down to your face, the back of your head and neck. You're starting to drift off. You are feeling very relaxed."

Honute listened to Akila and let her guide him to the land of sleep. On one level he was aware of everything in the room. He could sense that Theoris was off to the right, just behind Akila. He could smell Akila's scent of lilac and honey. Even Theoris' scent came through. It was the smell of glycerin soap, unscented, then he smelled a hint of honeydew and rose. A combination Hypatia enjoyed. On the other level he knew he was saying things that didn't make sense. It was a string of jumbled words with no meaning. Some would call it speaking in Tongues, he called it

127

babbling.

Akila took Honute deep. It amazed her how quickly he went under. Usually it took several sessions to get a person that deep.

Theoris passed Akila a note. It said, "Ask him about the war."

Akila swallowed dry. She took a deep breathe and said, "Honute, can you hear me?"

Honute nodded.

"I want you to lift you right arm up and hold there."

He did.

"I want you to image that your arm is not your arm and you feel no sensation. Do you understand? Repeat what I asked you?"

Honute did. He understood perfectly.

Akila reached out and pinched him a nasty bruise.

He did not winch.

"Put you arm down."

He did.

"I want you to float back to a time you were not a priest. Go back to when the war was with the Cursed Lands. Do you understand?"

Honute frowned, but nodded.

"I want you to tell me of a time during the war where you engaged the enemy."

Honute was still for a moment.

Theoris watched in fascination. She scribbled on the pad of paper and passed Akila another note.

Akila read it and looked at her.

Theoris nodded.

Akila took another deep breathe and let it out slowly.

Honute said, "Shhhhh."

And Akila nearly jumped.

Honute said, "The enemy is here and I see them. There are about twelve of them, coming up the hill. Shhhhh. Hold still. Maybe they might pass."

The room was still and neither woman moved.

Honute frowned. "There, one of them. Curse him, he spotted

us." Then Honute yelled out, "Engage!"

Akila jumped. "Tell me what is happening."

Honute was breathing heavy. "They are running up the hill and coming at us. Some of my men are hit. I shoot one, a dozen times but he is still coming. They must be hyped on STIM. I pull out some grenades and I toss them. Bodies and pieces of bodies are everywhere. That stopped them, but something is wrong. No, this is not right." Honute started to become agitated.

Akila said, "Honute, relax. Listen to my voice. Do you hear me?"

After a tense moment Honute nodded.

Akila said, "What is wrong. Tell me, but you will remain calm. Do you understand?"

Honute nodded. "This did not happen."

Akila looked at Theoris.

Theoris scribbled a note and gave it Akila.

Akila read it. "Honute, listen to my voice. When you hear my voice it will relax you. You will not fear anything. Do you understand me?"

Honute nodded. "I will not fear anything."

"Look at the plants. Are they real?"

Honute hesitated. "They are plants."

Akila pressed forward. "Are they real?"

Honute paused. His forehead wrinkled heavily.

Akila pressed forward again. "Are they real, Honute? I need you to tell me if the plants are real."

For a long moment Honute was silent.

Akila was about to say something when Theoris rested her hand on Akila's shoulder.

Akila turned to look and Theoris placed a finger to her lips. Akila nodded, turned to look back at Honute and waited.

After several minutes Honute spoke. "The plants are not real."

Akila turned to Theoris.

Theoris wrote something out.

Akila took the note and stared at it. She swallowed hard. "Are the bodies real?"

Honute drew in a long breathe. He slowly said, "Yes." And then screamed.

Akila jumped.

Honute grabbed at the couch edge and dug his fingers in deep. The fabric ripped.

Akila said, "Listen to my voice, Honute."

Honute stopped screaming.

"What happened? Tell me, what do you see?"

Honute relaxed and seemed to give in to whatever he had been fighting. "I see death. I killed."

"With the grenades?"

Honute shook his head. "With my hands. All of them. I killed them all. Murdered them as they stood in front of me."

Akila and Theoris were shocked.

Honute continued. "I tortured them like they did me. They will never touch a single thing again. I don't want to be here."

"Okay, Honute, come back to me."

Honute relaxed again, smiled, and said, "Dr. Theoris has some of Hypatia on her."

Theoris blushed deep red.

Honute said, "I smell Hypatia's scent, it is nice. Theoris should wear more of it."

Theoris quickly scribbled on the pad and handed the whole thing to Akila.

Akila looked back and Theoris nodded. "Honute, listen to my voice. Tell my how you feel about Hypatia."

Honute went silent for a few seconds. "That bitch. The selfish prissy bitch is always nagging. Thoth how I want to shut her up sometimes, but I can't."

"Why is that?"

"I am no longer a warrior. I am a simple humble priest who wants to help people. I have to help people because it will make me feel better."

Theoris' eyes widened. She took the pad from Akila and

scribbled. She gave the pad back.

It read, "What will make you sad?"

"Honute frowned deeply, "Killing people." He started to cry. "I don't want to see people die. It hurts and I feel bad."

Theoris leaned forward and whispered in Akila's ear.

Akila said, "Honute, listen to my voice. You will remember the plants to be real. You will remember that you had a wonderful nap and you heard non-sense words. Do you understand me?"

Honute nodded. "I understand. The plants are real. Theoris really should wear more of the perfume. I think it smells better on her. I had a wonderful nap and I heard non-sense words."

Akila leaned forward. "Honute, wake up." She reached out and shook his shoulder.

Honute opened his eyes and stretched. He yawned loudly and arched his back. "Did it work? What is that wonderful scent?" He sniffed the air and smiled. "Did I do anything silly?"

Akila and Theoris forced a smile.

Theoris said, "Honute, you and Akila did well. You have helped a lot."

Honute beamed and stretched. He liked helping people. It made him feel better. "I am glad." He smiled was deep and wide. He did feel good.

Chapter 22

Rivota sat across the table and talked in between chewing. Theoris would never have thought it possible, but Rivota could talk and breathe simultaneously. The woman just wouldn't shut up. On and on and on she talked, through the lunch, through four cups of coffee, right down to desert. Then Rivota said, "So, how are you and Hypatia doing?"

Theoris, at first, wanted to choke her. She decided not. She'd never get away with it. Too many witnessed. She sipped at her own cup of coffee. "What do you mean?"

Rivota laughed and her whole body shook. "It is okay. Half the facility knows and the other half doesn't care. Except for Dr. Funutsu, he's had a crush on Dr. Hypatia for months now. It nearly tore his heart out when he found out."

Theoris definitely wanted to choke her out. She wondered if she could bribe everyone in the cafeteria. Then she remembered the cameras. She could yell fire and in the ensuing stampede she could yank Rivota's vocal cord out. "Again I ask you, what do you mean?" She took another sip.

Rivota studied Theoris' face for a moment. She nodded and smile. "I like you Theoris. You got a nice poker face. No more questions about that then. But I should tell you that Dr. Hypatia had been visiting one of my interns for some time. About a week ago she suddenly stopped. He was concerned and that made me wonder. For about three months she would find her way down to the medical area to visit. Sometimes they both would disappear for a few hours, sometimes it was for only a few minutes. Her suddenly stopping meant that that yummy husband of hers was back in action or she found someone else. I really hate being left in the dark about things. So I just sat back and watched." She let Theoris think about that one.

Theoris sipped at her coffee and blinked.

Rivota smiled ago and sat back. "Can you get into shorter older women?"

"Pardon?"

"I may look fat, but I'm pretty solid. I can bench nearly two hundred and I jog about three miles a day." When Theoris still didn't get it Rivota said, "So, I guess I'm asking if you'd like to go out to dinner sometime?"

Theoris nearly choked on the coffee, but she caught it and squelched the cough in time. She sipped again and blinked at Rivota. What an interesting turn of events happening she thought. "You've placed me in an unexpected position. I don't know how to answer that question."

Rivota drank a mouth full of coffee and nodded. "That's okay. No need to answer now, but if you do decide give me a call. You have my number?"

Theoris nodded. She had everyone's home number who was involved in the project.

Rivota looked at her timepiece. "Time to go. Dr. Ohyutri is guest speaker. He's made some pioneering work in biotechnology. Do you want me to have the session taped?"

Theoris nodded and said "Thanks, I would appreciate it." Damn this woman she thought. She knew she had a weakness for biotech. 'Curse you!' was what she wanted to say. Instead, she mustered up a very believable "Okay, you enjoy it and give me all the good details."

Rivota smiled, got up, and left.

Theoris sipped the last drop out of the cup and thought. 'A very most interesting turn of events.'

Honute tried to settle himself as best as he could. He was strapped down and inclined in the middle of several scary looking pieces of equipment. Theoris explained that the devices would be measuring the magnetic field around him. They would only detect changes. He still worried because they vaguely reminded him of something from his past. He couldn't pinpoint what it was, but the entire arrangement made his stomach knot up.

Akila sat in the monitoring room watching all the equipment recorders. The Physics department turned one of the storage rooms into a makeshift sensory deprivation chamber. She watched Honute on one of the monitors and wished she could be there. She could tell that he was a bit uncomfortable. She watched a line on one of the screens jump erratically. She flipped the microphone switch on. "Honute, how are you feeling?" And on a whim she said, "Honute, do you hear my voice?"

Honute felt terrible. This was the first time in a long time he could remember where he didn't feel in control of himself. He tried to compose himself but it was like the machines were caving in on him. The last thing he wanted was to panic, but he was balanced on the edge and he couldn't stop. Then he heard Akila's voice. It was like a goddess calling to him. He felt the panic subside and it was no longer crowded. "I'm doing fine." He released the breath he had been holding.

Theoris was standing behind Akila when one of the recorders went trippy. She watched with an intellectual eye as the squiggly line straightened out.

Ayruyi sat in the corner waiting patiently for everyone to finish. She was thinking about what to cook for dinner and was torn between a traditional meal of mutton and lamb, and one of those dishes she learned to make in the Far East. High Priest Ferruk had made her learn how to prepare a specialty dish of sliced raw fish and rice balls. She was reluctant to admit it but she enjoyed the dish and she found herself wondering if Master Honute would enjoy it. She let herself daydream while everyone else worked – she was beginning to enjoy being Master Honute's servant. Her thoughts stopped just short of wanting to rid herself of Master Ferruk. Servants are dealt with harshly and slowly for killing a master, regardless on whether it is in self-defense or not.

Akila said, "Relax. This is going to take a few minutes."

Honute's image on the monitor nodded.

Theoris noted everything and was about to settle down for a few seconds when she noticed Honute frowning.

Honute suddenly smelt a fragrance he hadn't smelled in a week or so. It was unmistakably. It was Hypatia's perfume.

Akila noticed the recorders squiggle wildly. An alarm went off.

Hypatia stood in the door way. She froze when she heard the alarm. Moments later the alarm stopped.

Theoris turned around. "Dr. Hypatia. Nice of you to join us."

Hypatia nodded. "Am I in the way?"

Theoris walked over and flipped the on switch to the mike. She shook her head. "Not at all."

Honute sat in his silent box and waited. He still smelled Hypatia's perfume. He loved that smell. He had been thinking about buying Akila a bottle. Then he heard, "Not at all. Sit over here." He thought it odd, but figured either Theoris or Akila didn't want him to feel lonely. He was just at the edge of falling asleep when he heard Hypatia's voice. Something in him burned and he felt warm.

Hypatia sat in one of the chairs behind a monitor. She watched Honute's image. Her heart thum-rumped and she sighed. "How is everything working out? Is he working out?"

Theoris pulled a chair beside her, to the left. She could see Honute's image and the one of the monitors with the squiggly activity. She looked over to Akila and gave her the "don't say anything" gesture – index finger to lips.

Akila nodded and hoped Theoris knew what she was doing.

A knock at the door had everyone turn. Ferruk, a bodyguard and an old man stood in the doorway.

Ayruyi jumped up and approached Ferruk. "Master Ferruk. Master Honute has treated me well. I am here waiting to serve him as you have instructed."

Ferruk smiled. "My lovely Ayruyi, I do hope you have missed me. I am glad he is treating you well."

Ayruyi felt guilty and blushed. Ferruk decided the blush an affirmative to her missing him. Ayruyi knew it to be guilt and shame. Guilt that she should have missed Ferruk, and shame that she would miss Honute instead. She bowed her head deep, "Of course Master Ferruk. I have missed you terribly."

Ferruk puffed out his chest and walked up to Theoris. "How goes everything, Theoris. Any progress yet?"

Theoris forced a smile and doubled her effort to make her voice sound congenial. "We just started to run some tests." She pointed to the monitors. "We're testing for any changes to the electromagnetic field around him."

Ferruk frowned. "Electromagnetic field? Explain in simpler terms." He commanded.

Theoris bit her lip until it bleed. "The aura around us. We want to measure that."

Ferruk said, "Ahhh, that I understand. Simpler terms are better." He looked around the room and rested his eyes on Hypatia. He smoothly walked over to her.

Theoris near rage decided choking him would not be in her best interest. She added his name to the list of people who further pissed her off. She introduced the two. "This is Dr. Hypatia. Honute's wife."

Ferruk paused and thought for a moment. "And what a lovely creature you are – Hypatia, if you don't mind me calling you that?"

Hypatia smiled and nearly gushed. "Not at all, High Priest Ferruk."

"Please, call me Ferruk. I am at your service."

Theoris winced. "She is in charge of the Astrophysics department."

Ferruk chuckled, "And brilliant, too." He decided not to touch this one. Not in respect of a fellow priest, but that smart women turned him off. He looked around noting everything and everyone. "So, when do we see something?"

Akila smiled as she watched the squiggly lines jerk up and down, squiggle and bounce all over the paper.

Hypatia looked at the monitor. "High . . . Ferruk, my husband is but a humble and simple priest. I don't think he could be anything more important than performing his daily tasks."

Ferruk raised an eyebrow. He looked Hypatia in the eyes and blinked everyone else in the room out. "I can hear it in your voice. You don't approve of daily chores?"

She smiled and stared back, "If you have no ambition then I suppose one would be made perfectly for the job." She turned to see Honute's image on a nearby monitor. "I do hope that the project works out and that it is not sabotaged by Honute's passivity."

"Sabotaged?!? By passivity? Really?" Ferruk asked.

Theoris almost gasped.

Hypatia wondered how Theoris would feel if she maneuvered her way into Ferruk's heart. He was no Honute and she was sure he could only put out a little bit as best. "Honute doesn't like confrontation. That is one of the most damaging flaw of his personality. I'm afraid small birds and kids would be better suited for this project.

Ferruk and Hypatia laughed.

Everyone else was silent. Then an alarm went off. Then another and another. A few seconds later all the alarms went off.

Hypatia looked at Honute's image and swore he flashed a scowl at her.

Ferruk said loudly, "What is going on?"

Theoris hid her smile and felt elated that Honute was provoked into a response. She figured his ability was connected to his emotions. She let the scene play out. Theoris turned to Akila and nodded.

Akila leaned over to the mike and said. "Honute, can you hear me?"

A second later the room went silent and everyone turned to Akila.

She blocked them out of her mind and continued, "Honute. You can relax now."

All the squiggly lines went straight.

That fact did not escape Ferruk. He smiled and said, "Interesting. When can you give me a report?"

Theoris almost pouted. "We'd have to collect and analyze all the data."

Ferruk shot her an exasperated look. "How about I make it easy on you. I'll be contacting Pharaoh in four hours. You have three to do what you people do to come up with at least some type of answer." He didn't wait for Theoris to respond. Ferruk turned on his heels and walked out. The body guard and old man followed.

Hypatia remained silent for a moment. She decided to say as little as possible. "I'll meet with you later. If you need anything don't hesitate to call." She turned and walked out before Theoris' obvious cloudy mood erupted into a storm.

Chapter 23

Ferruk sat at Theoris' desk. Theoris was furious. If it wasn't for the bodyguard squeezed in one of the corners she'd kill Ferruk, possibly splay him and hang what was loose out the window. The old man had walked in with a tray. A coffee pot, cups and pastry was on top. The old man, Theoris later learned was Ayruyi's father, placed the tray on the desk. He poured coffee into the cup and measured out an exact amount of honey and cream into one of the cups. He sipped at it, waited a moment, and then handed it to Ferruk.

Ferruk took it and took a swallow. He smiled at Theoris. "Are you sure you don't want a cup? Arrutyi makes a very decent cup."

Theoris said, "I'd like my desk back."

Ferruk smiled and leaned back in her chair. "The years have been good to you, Theo –"

"You may not call me that, I gave –"

"You gave me nothing!" He flung the report at her head, but it missed. "I need something better to give to Pharaoh. This, this, this report you gave is written in incomprehensible gibberish. Pharaoh could not possibly understand."

Theoris finished counting to ten. "Pharaoh very well could understand it, as he has understood many of the other projects this University has produced." She poked at the air and toward Ferruk with her middle finger. "You can't understand it."

Ferruk slammed his hand on the table and swept the contents on the desk on the floor.

Theoris jumped up, but stopped.

The bodyguard had appeared at the edge of the desk.

Theoris sat back down.

Arrutyi walked over to the fallen contents and started to pick them up.

Ferruk, without moving his eyes from Theoris, said, "Leave them. Fetch me a fresh cup of coffee."

"Yes, Master." The old man said. The coffee appeared in less than a minute.

Ferruk sipped at the cup. "Tell me in simple words what happened." He leaned back into the chair.

Theoris looked at her stuff on the floor, then the bodyguard, then Ferruk. "Honute changed the electromagnetic field around him. We don't know how – well, actually we do but I can't tell you in simple terms or of what importance this is. When the program started we didn't know what would happen."

"But you had some idea, yes?" He sipped his coffee some more.

"Yes. Maybe telekinesis –"

"That's moving things from a distance?"

Theoris nodded. "Yes. Maybe, affect the magnetic field, as Honute has. Maybe able to change nearby ambient temperatures."

"And this magnetic field changing? What could it be used for?"

"Maybe affect other electromagnetic fields. He might be able to direct a concentrated field –"

"Like a blue bolt?" Ferruk interrupted.

Theoris gave him an inquisitive look. She nodded. "We are still testing."

Ferruk had an unfocused gaze. He seemed to have mentally wandered off. A moment later he returned. "After the alarms started going off, your lovely assistant said something to Honute. What was it?"

"She told him to relax."

"And that was all."

Theoris nodded.

"You know that Honute was a soldier."

Theoris held her composure and nodded.

"A very successful, yet violent one."

She nodded again.

Ferruk smiled. "Why would you give something as this to such a man?"

Theoris took a deep breath. "We didn't know until after we began."

Ferruk thought about that for a moment. He sipped at the coffee. A minute later a laugh started. It rumbled from deep within his chest and came out loud and long. It went on for a minute and slowly subsided. "You didn't know? All priest are humble creatures. Was that it? If it worked he could be controlled? Is that what she did, gave him a hypnotic suggestion?" He laughed again. "That I totally understand. Let me think for a few minutes. Wait outside until I'm done."

Theoris sat.

Ferruk looked over to her and frowned.

Theoris said, "This is my office."

Ferruk smiled, "For the moment, no." He looked at the bodyguard.

He nodded, walked over to Theoris. He hovered menacingly.

"You can either leave on your own, or you can leave by . . . ."

Theoris got up. She slammed her door shut on the way out. She stood by the doorway for a moment, fuming and plotting. Then an idea hit her. She burst into laughter but squelched it quickly and hurried to find Honute and Akila. She had a surprise for High Priest Ferruk, Friend of Pharaoh, Bastard to everyone else.

Chapter 24

Ayruyi watched Akila out of the corner of her eye. Both women were in the kitchen making dinner. Honute had to put his foot down and tell Ayruyi to let Akila in there. Akila wanted to make a fig cake. She said it was a desert passed down from generation to generation in her family. Honute inched toward her and asked how long she wanted him to hold the cake under water. Akila looked perplexed. Honute inched his way toward the exit and said, "I figure it is rock hard by now. How old is that cake?" Akila and Honute both laughed. She told him to get out and stay out. Ayruyi had witnessed the whole shameless act of two lovers getting to know each other. One would tell a bad joke, the other would laugh like it was the funniest thing said. Ayruyi fumed over Akila's smile and free spirited laugh. She likened it to freedom and wished she had it. She turned back to trimming pieces off a lamb shank. The knife blade neatly slicing off long thin silvers of fat and meat. She dropped into a trance and worked the knife automatically. All her life she dreamt of being free with kids, a house, and a husband, the perfect life and all the things that came with it. It was a favorite dream, with all the noises and sights she learned to weave with many years of practice. However, the man never had a face. His face was almost non-descript with the eyes, nose, and mouth a-sometimes-out-of-focus collection of parts, never sharpening to crystal clarity. He never had a face in all those years until today. The face was that of Honute, her temporary master, literally the man of her dreams. She was nearly done when her dream was broken by a happy Akila humming sweetly out loud. Ayruyi wheeled on Akila with a speed that would have intimidated her had she not been absently mindful of sweet nothings. Ayruyi felt her arm snap out and plunge the knife deep in Akila's back. It made a wet tearing sound as it sliced through muscle and floating ribs.

Akila screamed sharply and grabbed at her back.

Ayruyi removed the knife and stared at Akila. On one level she was glad to have done it because Akila would die soon and Honute would be free to love her. On another level she was frightened because Akila would die soon and Honute would be angry. A wave of guilt and shame surrounded her like cold fingers of despair. She choked out a cry and wept. "Oh Goddess Isis, what have I done!"

Honute ran in and saw blood flowing from Akila's back.

Ayruyi stopped crying and turned toward Honute. She stepped over Akila and said, "Master, I am sorry. I did this because I love you. Don't punish me."

Honute stood frozen at the scene, Akila bleeding on the floor and Ayruyi pleading not to be punished. "What have you done?" He yelled, a temper he hadn't felt in years sprung from somewhere deep inside him. He went to help Akila when Ayruyi thrusted the knife in front of him.

"I love you." Ayruyi yelled. "I did this for you!" It sounded like so much desperation that it even sickened Ayruyi.

Honute grabbed her wrist and tossed her sideways into the far wall.

Ayruyi hit it like a doll and collapsed to the floor. "I did it for you, Master" Tears flowed down her cheeks. "I did it for you. Can't you see that?"

Honute ignored her and pressed firmly on the flowing wound.

Ayruyi pounded the floor with fists and yelled, "I did this for you. You are the one I love. I did this for you."

Honute turned and yelled, "Shut up and call for help!"

Ayruyi looked at her master caring over Akila. Anger replaced shame, rage replaced guilt. She got up and ran toward Honute.

Honute sensed her charge before he saw it. Instinctively, his foot shot back and hit Ayruyi square in the chest.

Ayruyi lost her wind and clinched her chest. Honute's foot would leave a very nasty bruise. She collected herself and lunged.

Honute turned with his hand outstretched. He braced himself as he knew the blade would slip cleanly through it. As the blade touched his skin the entire metal splatted to the ground in a semi-solid mass.

Ayruyi stopped and stared. Honute, stunned, stared also. He looked at his hand and began to wonder. Ayruyi watched the play of emotions on his face, a seemingly random montage of distortion.

Honute felt that different something again. The first time was at the hospital. This was the second. He held his breathe and knelt next to Akila. She was already unconscious. Something urged him to place his hand on her now trickling wound. He pressed hard and felt burning energy seep from and through his fingers. Little prickling pulses sliced along the surface of his skin and he "saw" a soft green glow cover his hand. It grew brighter and brighter as the burning sensation became almost unbearable. Then as quickly as it started it was gone. He lifted his hand away and stood up. He looked down at Akila and said, "Rise."

Akila opened her eyes and saw Honute staring down at her. His lovely robe was covered in blood but he was smiling at her. He told her to "rise." She felt a receding throb of pain where the knife wound had been. It all happened fast. She reached around and felt the torn and sliced through clothing but didn't feel the gaping wound. She reached up and let Honute lift her to her feet, "How?" She asked.

Honute smiled and said, "By Thoth's will and power. By his will and power I tell you. He has manifested in me the power to heal." His eyes welled up. "I can do this. I can help the sick in Thoth's name."

Akila watched Honute. She was proof that something miraculous happened. She looked at the melted mass of metal at Honute's feet and an Ayruyi on the floor.

Ayruyi looked up with tears in her eyes. She saw the miracle. Her master healed Akila in witness to her eyes. She repositioned herself and knelt in front of Honute. "Oh, Master Honute, Healing

Priest, I bow to you my humble form and give you my life. I witnessed the miracle of power and you are my living god, the embodiment of Ra, Horus, Osiris, Pharaoh." She started giggling. It was slow and soft, then built up to a frightening hysteria of laughter. She tore her clothes off in a crazed possessed way and rubbed Akila's blood over her body. She screamed out, "I am witness to a new god. Glory be to the mighty Master Honute. Honute-Ra I say! Honute-Ra!"

Honute was shocked. He grabbed at Ayruyi's thrashing body as it tried to cover itself in blood.

She screamed again. "Honute-Ra! Honute-Ra! I am your slave. Command me." She laughed wildly and embraced Honute in a passionate hold. She sobbed and laughed and giggled and moaned and rubbed herself against him. She screamed out loud again as she reached an orgasm. Its intensity enveloped her in a crash of intense convulsions. It peaked within seconds and she blacked out.

Honute sat there holding a passed out Ayruyi, who was moaning and giddy at the same time.

Akila knelt beside him. "Is she all right?"

He nodded. Then the realization hit him. Ayruyi's reaction may not be so unusual. It hit him harder. Suppose others react the same way. His mind raced and he felt dizzy. "Oh Thoth, what have you done!"

Akila looked at Honute and said, "What do you mean?"

He placed his blood covered hand to his forehead. "All is lost. They're going to treat me like a god. This is going to be a curse."

Then it hit Akila. Honute was right. The other shoe just dropped.

Ayruyi woke up in bed. She had a bad dream and was glad it was only a dream. It was about how she tried to murder Akila and that Honute had turned into a god. She stretched and yawned and had wondered how she got here. Then she got scared and jumped out of bed. She was in Master Honute's bed. Even though he was a wonderful master and kind and caring he would surely punish her for being in his bed. She looked around and noted nothing out of place. Then she thought maybe the Master had bedded her. She smiled at the thought and tried to dredge up the moment. Nothing was there. She frowned and sat on a nearby chair. Something had to have happened to have her sleeping in his bed, but the only thing that kept coming to mind was that horrible dream. The one with her holding a knife and thrusting it in the Akila's back and then her attacking Honute and witnessing him disarm her and then healing Akila. She remembered an overwhelming erotic feeling come over her. It was like she went mad and sensuality overtook and controlled her body. The words of her chanting Honute-Ra surfaced and she had a sinking feeling that it wasn't a dream. She walked to the door, opened it, looked out and saw no one. She stepped out into the hallway and stopped at the living room entry. She saw Honute and Akila curled up in a sheet next to the fire. Both seemed to be naked. Tears welled up and she started to cry as she realized it was not a dream. She ran to the two and collapsed at their feet. "Master Honute, Personage Akila, forgive me, please."

Honute woke with a start and saw Ayruyi run toward him. She dropped to her knees, crying.

Akila opened her eyes to see Ayruyi begging for forgiveness. She kept going on and on about how sorry she was.

Ayruyi cried and bowed, all the while apologizing. "I am so sorry. So sorry."

Honute sat up and the sheet fell away from him. He was exposed.

Ayruyi blushed and looked away. No longer can she bear witness to Master Honute-Ra, her god. Shame had overcome her as she remembered she wanted to make love to him just the day before. Her body shivered as she thought about the consequences for such a thought. Gods are to be worshiped and loved, not scandalously lusted over for erotic gratification. She was appalled at herself. She bowed faster and begged louder.

Honute stood up, but didn't think about his nudity. "Ayruyi!" He snapped.

Ayruyi, startled, shut up. She stared down at the carpet, rocking back and forth.

Akila got up and placed a hand over Ayruyi's shoulder.

Ayruyi shrank inward and cried harder.

Akila held her and whispered in her ear. "It is okay Ayruyi. I forgive you. Stop crying."

Through tear covered vision Ayruyi saw a divine beauty in Akila. Akila was the most beautiful woman in all the Blessed Lands and she would do anything to show her worthiness to be in her favor. She had done the worst offense to this personage and now she was forgiven. Ayruyi swore she would protect Akila with her life. She stopped crying.

Akila said, "Good that's better. Are you feeling better?"

Ayruyi nodded and wiped away the tears. Her eyes puffy and red now, she said the only really decent thing, she believed at this moment, to say. "How may I serve you, Personage Akila?"

Akila smiled, hugged her and said. "I am glad you are doing okay. I was worried."

Tears started to well up in Ayruyi's eyes again and her bottom lip started to shake. Shame and a sense of unworthiness started to descend over her.

Akila said, "Stop it. No more tears," as she started to lift Ayruyi up.

Honute, in a robe now, moved to the side and helped lift Ayruyi.

Ayruyi nearly passed out from his touch.

Akila shooed him off with instructions to bring Ayruyi something to drink.

Ayruyi's heart skipped a beat. Personage Akila ordered Master Honute to the kitchen to do domestic work. All was lost she felt.

Akila placed her on the couch. "Ayruyi, I do forgive you."

Ayruyi stared as long as she dared into Akila's eyes. She hoped that the Personage was not trying to trick her. She nodded.

Chapter 25

Hypatia had been furious. If this had been her house she would have tossed breakable furniture across the room.

Theoris sat and watched with a certain dred that is onset when one realizes that a mistake had been made. She witnessed Hypatia throwing a tantrum. She wasn't on all fours kicking and screaming but that would not have made a difference. The result was the same. She looked silly in Theoris' eyes, and that was close to a relationship death sentence.

Hypatia burnt herself out and sat down in a huff. She looked at Theoris and regretted her childish outburst. She couldn't help it. They just happened, but at least this time, she had the regardfulness to keep her hands off the breakables. "I'm sorry. I feel silly."

Theoris nodded but said nothing.

Hypatia felt a momentary rush of anger but squelched it quickly. "Anyway, I was just upset that I won't be able to go with you."

Theoris told Hypatia that Pharaoh had invited her to the palace for a special dinner. He wanted to met Honute and personally discuss, with her, the ramifications of her research success. It was a big deal and Hypatia was going to miss out because of her separation from Honute. He got one, Theoris got one, and so did Akila, which bite deeply into Hypatia's skin. Ayruyi was also going, as Honute's guest.

Hypatia cursed Akila, though she really hadn't known the woman. She never considered getting to know her. Now that it looked like Honute was finally becoming something she was on the outside. She kicked herself for being selfish. If only she had waited a few more weeks and just endured. "How long are you going to be gone?"

Theoris said, "Probably a few days. Ferruk will be escorting us and he wants to take the rail."

Hypatia simply said, "Oh."

After several moments of silence Theoris said, "How about I finally take you to that Greek restaurant?"

Hypatia perked up. She smiled sweetly and Theoris completely forgot about the tantrum.

Both women collected their things and walked out the door.

Honute, Akila and Ayruyi sat in the taxi as it drove to the Greek Marble. Honute was in high spirits. He and Akila had been invited to sit with Pharaoh. Akila was particularly thrilled as she had never ventured too far from New Heliopolis. Ayruyi took it as a normal day. Being a servant to one of the most powerful men in the Blessed Lands brings her in contact with many powerful and wealthy persons. Pharaoh was one of them, particularly since her mother and father had been in service with Pharaoh before her mother passed. The taxi pulled up to the front entrance of the Greek Marble. Honute paid the driver and all three got out and walked in. The host recognized Honute and Akila and ushered them in to one of the choice seats.

Ayruyi loved Greek food. She told Honute that she could make it. Her mother taught her. She said that her family lineage can be traced to Greece, before it was conquered by Egypt and its people enslaved.

Honute nodded and replied, "One day we will cook together. You can show me how to prepare some of your favorite dishes. But today you eat with us."

Ayruyi pouted and followed. She really wasn't all that disappointed. Honute-Ra and Personage Akila were taking her out to dinner. What more could a servant ask for?

Theoris pulled into the parking lot of the Greek Marble and parked the car. She and Hypatia walked into the restaurant and waited for the Host to seat them. He told them that a table would be available in a few moments, but if they would like they could have a seat at the bar to pass the time away. Theoris looked at Hypatia. This was the first time the two had been out in a while. The last time she made the decisions, this time she deferred to Hypatia.

Hypatia said, "Maybe a drink would be nice."

The Host smiled and led them to the bar.

The barkeep stepped up and placed napkins before them. "Okay Ladies, what would you like?"

Theoris said, "Give me a Kourtakis."

"And you, Miss?" The barkeep asked.

Hypatia thought for a bit. "I don't know. Something sweet, but not to sweet."

The barkeep smiled. "I have just the thing for you." He stepped away and after a few moments came back with a glass of wine in one hand and a tall thin glass with a clouded blue liquid in the other.

Hypatia looked at it. She sniffed the contents, took a sip and smiled. "Yummy, what is it called."

The barkeep smiled. "The perfect man. Tall, good looking, sweet, but with some bite, slips in smoothly, and leaves a pleasant feeling when you are done."

Hypatia laughed and took a bigger sip.

The Host can up and said, "Your table is ready."

Both women followed him into the dining room.

Hypatia thought she heard Honute's voice. She stopped in her tracks when she realized it was Honute. She heard a young woman's voice, then she heard Honute laugh. It had been a long time since she heard him laugh. It was a full hearty laugh that was infectious to those around him.

Theoris heard it to. She recognized Akila's voice and a sinking feeling developed in the pit of her stomach. She gave Hypatia a sideway glance and braced herself.

Hypatia followed the Host to a table. They walked up to a laughing Honute and Akila. Ayruyi was quiet but smiling.

Honute was in a good mood. Akila had just finished telling a story about her first time meeting Theoris. She said that the Doctor had just finished ripping a new hole in the Chairman of the board. She had yanked him by the tie and told him she was tired of the bullshit and for them to hurry up and hire or promote someone in the Astrophysics department. She said that he looked all choked up and his face was a beet red. Theoris released the necktie, turned and in a very sweet voice said. "Hi, you must be my new intern. Don't mind him, he's my boss. Let's go talk." Honute laughed and a moment later he saw Theoris and Hypatia walk toward them.

Theoris stopped and said, "Akila, Honute." She looked at Ayruyi, nodded and then back to Honute and Akila.

Honute stood up and acknowledged both women. "Dr. Theoris, Hyp, it is a surprise to see you here."

Hypatia looked at the women and then at Honute, "No doubt. We won't ruin your dinner." She straightened her back, lifted her chin and walked passed them.

Theoris shrugged, "I'll talk to you guys later," and followed the Host and Hypatia to the table.

For a long time, no one said anything. Glasses of wine had been poured, dinner served, silent chewing.

Theoris and Hypatia sat in silence.

Hypatia's glass was nearly drained when the waiter appeared. She finished the glass and asked for another. She had a clear view of the back of Honute's head with Akila on one side and Ayruyi on the other. She fumed and stewed and sucked down half the drink on one swallow. She wondered which one Honute was doing, then she got angry because she thought that he may be doing both. The waiter came by and dropped off a third glass. The meal arrived a few minutes after that.

Honute felt Hypatia's burning gaze at his neck. He went through some mental exercises and relaxed visibly. He looked at

Akila and then at Ayruyi. He smiled broadly and lifted his glass of wine. He toasted, "To two very lovely and beautiful women. May Thoth watch over all three of us." He took a drink. Akila and Ayruyi smiled and drank.

Ayruyi was keenly aware that something was not right. This "Hyp" woman was very beautiful but seemed to have a problem with her Master and god. Ayruyi watched this woman out of the corner of her eye and decided that she was a bitch and she wouldn't like her. She kept staring intensely at Honute and that bothered her. If Master Honute got mad he could squish her like a bug. She had decided to ask Master Honute how well he knew her when Honute raised the glass up and made a toast. She blushed when he said 'beautiful and lovely women.' Master Priest Ferruk complimented her often but it was, she felt, just to pacify her. Most often she did not feel beautiful, or lovely. After that the evening turned jovial again.

Honute was determined to enjoy himself. It was not always his lot in life to dine with two lovely women, one his lover, the other his servant. And with his wife sitting at the next table irony had not escaped him. It was interesting that Hyp was with Dr. Theoris. Interesting indeed, but he pushed the thought aside. He could ask Dr. Theoris tomorrow about this happenstance.

Akila felt a twinge of anger. She kept seeing Hypatia staring at them, particularly her. It was a look that people used to try and intimidate others. Once she stared back, but Hypatia's was more intense and full of energy. Akila acted like Honute said something, then looked away. The truth was, she blinked first and that was bound to nag at her. She finished her glass and excused herself to the restroom.

A moment later Hypatia got up but took the long route to the restroom. Theoris watched her, Ayruyi saw her, Honute missed it. Theoris shook her head – the evening was about to be ruined.

Akila hummed to herself while she washed her hands. The evening had been going well until Theoris showed up with Hypatia.

Akila guessed the rumors had been true. She thought it kind of ironic that Theoris would be involved with Honute's wife. It was a bit weird actually. She and Honute being lovers and apparently Theoris and Hypatia seeing each other, that was something to think about. Akila was deep in thought when Hypatia walked up next to her. Her sudden appearance almost startled Akila.

Hypatia washed her hands and said "You're sleeping with my husband."

Akila was shocked. She turned to face Hypatia, who stood nearly at the same eye level. Akila replied, "And you're sleeping with my boss."

Hypatia squared off and gave Akila a push. Akila almost lost her footing on the smooth floor. Hypatia stepped forward and pushed her again. "I don't like whores."

Akila had never been in a situation like this. She was locked in indecision as what to do. She had never been much of a fighter and she heard all the rumors of Hypatia's temper.

Hypatia stepped forward again. "I think you're a whore who fucks other women's husbands. I should have the law lock you up." She pushed Akila hard against the wall. "Bitch." Hypatia balled her fists up and was about to hit Akila in the face when she felt a strong hand grasp her at the wrist. She turned around.

Ayruyi had Hypatia's wrist in a vice grasp. She was positive she didn't like this woman. And now that she threatened Personage Akila she was going to hurt her. "Leave Personage Akila alone." Ayruyi said while maneuvering between Hypatia and Akila. "Leave her alone or you'll have to deal with me."

Hypatia looked Ayruyi up and down and laughed. "Move, slave, I have business with this other whore." She pulled her wrist out of Ayruyi's hand.

Ayruyi stood her ground. "You have business with me."

Hypatia stepped back and swing upward. She figured an uppercut would knock her out nicely.

Ayruyi saw the blow coming a second before Hypatia thought about making it. She backhanded the punch aside.

Hypatia blinked several times. She stepped forward and kicked in.

Ayruyi blocked the kick with her knee. She snapped her foot out and caught Hypatia between the legs.

Hypatia doubled over and got an open palm in the eye. Her head snapped back from the blow and she saw stars.

Ayruyi said, "Leave Personage Akila alone. Next time I will murder you." Then because of years of training and servitude she added, "Most honorable lady."

Ayruyi and Akila quickly walked out.

Hypatia composed herself and walked over to the mirror. Yep, she told herself. 'The little bitch blackened my eye." She fluffed back her hair and walked out the bathroom. Hypatia felt people looking at her as she walked passed them. She briefly stopped at Honute's table and gave Akila and Ayruyi a dirty look. She continued past them and sat at her table.

Theoris watched wide-eyed and said, "What in the Blessed Lands happened?"

Hypatia frowned and looked at Ayruyi. "That little bitch hit me." She said it loud. A few guests turned in their sits to see what was going on. "Yes, you." She said looking at Ayruyi. "You hit me."

Honute stared at Ayruyi. "Is this true?"

Ayruyi nodded, "Yes Master Honute-Ra, I defended Personage Akila from her. She threatened the Personage's being."

All eyes went to Hypatia.

Hypatia sank inward. "It wasn't like that." She turned to one of the guest. "Who are you staring at? Eat your meal!"

The room fell silent. A thick blanket of uneasiness floated through the room.

Hypatia stood up and pointed to Akila. "This whore is sleeping with my husband!"

Theoris' jaw dropped open at the quick turn of events. She looked around and scudded down in her chair.

Hypatia shouted again. The anger igniting over her like she was soaked in gasoline. She grabbed a bottle of wine from a nearby table and flung it at Akila.

It was a split second. Honute's hand shot up and the bottle imploded. His hand glowing bright red.

All eyes were on Honute.

Honute quickly dropped his hand and said, "I think we should leave."

Akila nodded, but Ayruyi grinned. She told herself, 'Honute-Ra will crush you you bitch. Feel his power.'

Honute collected both women and started for the door.

Hypatia yelled and flung another bottle at them.

Honute deflected the object. It too imploded, but not before it stopped in mid flight.

Theoris noted everything that happened. In a way she hoped something like this would occur, but she rather it had been private. The rumors were going to fly now. Honute, Akila and Ayruyi disappeared out the door.

A few moments later the Host appeared. "I am terribly sorry ladies, but I will have to ask you to leave." Though he and others had witnessed something amazing he still had to maintain some sort of dignity. After all, this was the "Marble Greek."

Theoris poured ice into a towel and wrapped the small cubes tight. She walked out of the kitchen, through the hall and into the bedroom.

Hypatia was in bed fuming when Theoris came in with the makeshift icepack. She grabbed at it and placed it on her eye. "The little bitch. I'll have her arrested for battery."

Theoris frowned but said nothing.

Hypatia looked at her with the good eye. "What? She hit me."

Theoris said nothing but stared back.

Hypatia looked away momentarily then visibly recomposed herself and looked back at Theoris.

Both women held the stare for nearly a minute.

Theoris said, "You can stay the night, but tomorrow you leave."

She turned and walked out of the bedroom leaving a shaken Hypatia, blackened eye and bruised ego.

Chapter 26

Theoris sat across from Honute and Akila. The rail was smooth and, to Theoris, almost enjoyable. She watched the two with a bit of envy and jealousy, but also with some happiness. They really did look good together. Honute was happy and carefree. He gabbed on about the wonders of Thoth and Akila seemed to be mesmerized. She supposed at one point she was like that when she and Ferruk had been young lovers. It was almost painful, remembering the old memories and reliving a dead past. But looking at Ferruk now just curled her heart tight. She resisted being bullied into putting Honute under hypnosis, but the threat of bodily harm was in part the reason she changed her mind. This time, she put Honute under and gave him a series of suggestions. Separately, they meant nothing, strung in a special way, they'd trigger a cascaded response within Honute's psych that would pause Osiris himself.

Honute stared out the window and wondered. There was something he was supposed to do, but for the life of him he could not remember. He saw Akila's reflection in the window. She was asleep and looked peaceful, perfect, and beautiful. How he enjoyed gazing at her face and lately it made him feel more at peace. He got up and decided to walk the length of the rail. He was stiff from siting in the chair and his back ached. He crossed the threshold to the next car. It was about midnight and everything was still. He crossed into the other car and felt someone behind him. He turned and noticed no one. The rail rumbled on. It vibrated and slightly rolled under his feet. He reached the end of the rail. It was the storage car and held all the baggage, tools and supplies. Honute walked the distance to the end and stopped at the door. It was locked, which made sense. No reason to have a child or sleepy careless passenger open it, step off into turbulent air, and cut his trip short. Honute looked out the window and felt that presence again. He refocused his eyes and saw a reflection in the window. He wheeled around in time to take a blow to the jaw. He stepped back into the door and it opened. His attacker threw a punch. Honute sidestepped and allowed the attacker's momentum to carry him past the door threshold. Honute pushed him the rest of the way. He watched as the attacker landed on the rail. He tumbled over wood and steel and came to a rest bludgeoned.

Honute reached over and yanked the emergency stop cord. Any item not fastened down shifted forward. A moment later the rail stopped. Honute jumped out the back and ran toward the broken mass. He moved a limb to the side to reveal the face. It was one of Ferruk's bodyguards.

Theoris had drifted off to sleep an hour ago. She had started to dream when she was thrown forward into her chair straps. She surveyed the compartment and noticed Honute missing. "Where's Honute?" She cried out.

Akila jumped out her seat and hastily walked toward the end of the rail.

Ferruk and another bodyguard searched upfront.

Honute looked up and saw Akila and Theoris running toward him. Ayruyi wasn't too far behind.   He stood up and waited for them to run the distance.

Akila stopped and hugged him. "Honute, are you okay?"

He nodded, hugged her back, and looked toward Theoris. "He tried to kill me?"

Theoris said, "Who is he?" Then see looked at the dead man's dirty face and recognized him. She looked up at Honute. "Tried to kill you?"

Honute nodded. "I think. He attacked me and was about to push me out the back end. Luckily, Thoth, gave me the strength to overcome. Otherwise, he'd be looking down at me."

Ferruk and a bodyguard ran up to the group.

Theoris and Ayruyi stepped aside and allowed Ferruk to walk up to the body. He looked at the face then at Honute. He said, "What happened?"

Honute eyed Ferruk and spoke, "He tried to kill me, most high priest Ferruk."

Ferruk's face twisted up in rage. "How dare he." He turned to the other guard. "Check his possessions and see if you can find a reason for this."

The conductor of the rail ran up to Ferruk. He was out of breath. "Vizier Ferruk, are you harmed?"

"No, no, I'm not harmed."

The conductor looked around and said, "Then who stopped the –" He looked down and saw the busted up body. "Oh. I see." He turned to one of his men, several had appeared. "Get something to cover the body up and put it in something. Take some pictures before you pick up the body." Several of his staff jumped into action. He turned to his assistant. "Forward a radio message to base. Tell them all is well, but we had an accident. One of the passengers had an accident." The man nodded and ran back toward the rail. "Vizier Ferruk, if you don't mind. I'd like to get you to your destination on time." He waited.

Ferruk looked at Honute. "We'll get to the bottom of this, Honute. In the meantime I'll assign my best guard to watch over you."

Theoris stepped up from behind. "I thought he was one of your best guards."

Ferruk's jaw muscles worked themselves for a few seconds. "He was a new guard. From a very noble family. All my other guards have long ties with me and their loyalty has been tested many times. I don't know what he was trying to do –"

"Kill Honute." Theoris said.

"Possibly." Ferruk answered.

Several men ran up with cloth and a makeshift coffin. One had a camera and started snapping pictures.

Ferruk continued, "We really don't know what his motive was, but we will find out. I'll personally have the Police Chief investigate this."

Honute watched the men place the body in the coffin and walked it toward the rail. "I would like to pray over him remains."

Ferruk said, "What? Pray for this . . . this man. He tried to kill you?"

Theoris interjected, "Possibly."

Ferruk ignored her. "You really want to pray over this man?"

Honute nodded, "It is what I do. And maybe when he reaches the afterlife Anubis will truly see through the veil and grant him some peace. Whatever his motive was he must have felt it to be important. I can't fault a man for following his heart."

Ferruk frowned for a second. He searched Honute's face for signs of deception and treachery. He told himself that Honute was very sincere. He smiled to himself and bowed his head. "Even a priest of the lower orders has something to remind the Vizier of the Middle Regions." Ferruk turned and walked toward the rail. He was lost in thought and felt a ping of guilt. He squelched it once he got on the rail and out of sight of curious eyes. He cursed the bodyguard for being careless. But for Ferruk it was a win-win situation. If the guard had succeeded in killing Honute than it would open up the way for him to place his own hand picked person to undergo the treatment and it would void the Oracles prediction. If Honute had done as he had done then he could watch the surveillance cams for signs of his magick or if his violent past had caught up with him. Then he could possibly have him arrested. Either way, Ferruk felt in charge. He laughed out loud as he entered his personal compartment. He was feeling good and alive. He called to one of the guards and instructed them to bring Ayruyi to him. He was going to spend the rest of the trip occupied. Ayruyi told him that Honute had not touched her. He nodded at that but realized that Honute had Akila. It was his bad timing, that's all. Not her fault, really, though he told her she could have tried harder and that he was disappointed. Ayruyi had nodded but didn't seem to bother by it. Ferruk forgot his train of thought when she entered the compartment. He drank in her beauty and body and pulled himself out. "Take it." He commanded. "Honute would not use you, but I will enjoy you."

Ayruyi bent down dreading the entire idea of being with Ferruk. Her heart and loyalty had changed. It was with Honute now and it was Honute she had wished to be her master. But she figured that in due time Honute will realize his potential and crush Ferruk and that would be the end of that.

Ferruk moaned as Ayruyi handled him. He told himself that this was the best that she had ever done. She seemed to have had an aggressive edge, like she was mad. That excited him even more. Yes, indeed, he decided that this was going to be a very pleasant rail ride.

Honute knelt in front of the makeshift coffin. He was back in the end car. The irony hadn't escaped him. He rocked back and forth humming out a tome from the book of the dead. The incense at either end of the coffin burned an aroma of cedar and cherry wood. Wisps of smoke traveled the length of the coffin. Honute began.

Art thou come to taken away my heart-case which lives? My heart-case which lives shall not be given unto thee. As I advance, the gods hearken unto my propitiation prayer and they fall down on their faces whilst they are on their own land. The Osiris Nu, whose word is truth, says, "O thou land of the Sceptre! O thou White Crown of the divine form! O thou rest of the ferry-boat! I am the Child. Yay!"

Chapter 27

Ivoniyut meet them at the rail. A long and impressive looking limousine awaited just outside the rail station. Pharaoh had sent word ahead of time and made the arrangements himself. The entire station had been cleared and Pharaoh's personal guards had every entrance and exit guarded, blocked, and watched. He was determined that another attempt on Honute's life was not going to happen again. When Ferruk approached Ivoniyut and looked into the guard's eyes he knew this was a joyous day. One obstacle had been removed. Ferruk's life got better. He was feeling particularly virile at that moment and decided that Ayruyi would enjoy this evening. During the ride Ferruk noticed that Ayruyi sat close to Honute and Akila. It perturbed him that she seemed so comfortable around them. She even talked endlessly of everyday things. She offered, with Master Ferruk's permission of course, to show them the crystal carvings and the holy shrine of Ra – only a few may enter, but with Master Ferruk's influence and being the guest of Pharaoh they could get in. She talked about cooking Greek food and wanting to learn how to bake Akila's family's fig cakes. On and on the woman talked. Ferruk had never known her to string more than a half dozen words together. And how did she know about the Crystal carvings and holy shrine? And he never remembered her knowing how to cook Greek food. Before the trip ended Ferruk realized two things. Ayruyi was something more than a servant, and maybe, just maybe he wasn't a good master. In one week, Honute did what he could never have done, made Ayruyi talk openly. He watched as she laughed and smiled and just seemed at ease. He liked her smile and the way she laughed made him want to laugh. She actually knew some jokes! Then the old doubts entered his mind and he remembered why he treated her the way he did. He wouldn't admit it but he cared about and loved her. As the feelings intensified he treated her worse and worse hoping that they would go away. They never did, so he keep his wall up and made the relationship strictly master and servant. He thought of the things he was going to do to her when they settled in. She'd be punished for her disloyalty. And as his thoughts got darker and darker his penis got harder and harder. He had plans for her, big plans, plans she'd would never forget or easily forgive.

The limo pulled onto the open road escorted by a dozen half-track tanks and a fighter aeroflight squadron. Pharaoh's complex was another twenty minutes away, but it was so large that even at this distance it could easily be seen silhouetting the bright day sky. The original complex had been located on the other side of the river. Pharaoh was displeased with how the sun rose over the east mountain. It created a misshapen shadow over the complex through out most of the day. He had the entire area moved to its new location. Now the peak of the mountain had been placed to the right as the sun rose. The complex would bask in yellow golden sunlight through the entire day and with the complex edged up the river bank it made for a spectacular sunset. The Sun and Moon would dance on the surface of the river when high in the sky, the light reflected over the land giving it a magical shimmering effect. Pharaoh would walk the edge singing praises to the gods and enjoying the evening. On special nights he would dance in the Moon light amidst joyous music and twisting swaying youthful dancer bodies. The entire complex would fill the open spaces just to glimpse the living embodied god thank the Blessed Lands and its people.

The last few miles of the trip had citizens lined up along the road. Most of them waved as the limo and escort vehicles passed. Honute looked out and was nearly floored by the mass of waving arms.

He asked, "Are they out there for us?"

Ferruk, dry-mouth and as unenthusiastic as he could muster said, "They want to see you. There are rumors that you can do things."

Honute turned, blinking rapidly, said, "How'd they find out?"

Ferruk looked at the younger priest and noted he said 'How'd they find out?' He simply said, "Word travels. The Blessed Lands is not blessed for keeping secrets."

Honute turned back and watched the endless mass of people. It was overwhelming. He lay back in the seat and thanked Thoth he was inside and they were outside.

Ferruk had received some satisfaction in Honute's discomfort. He smirked.

The limo stopped in front of a grand arch. Huge statues of Anubis, the jackal headed god of the underworld, stood on either side on the arch opening. They were painted in bright earthy colors. Yellow and green for the clothing and olive-tan for the Anubis face. 'Pharaoh likened the entrance to the underworld because only the fateful and invited souls may enter in safety. All others have but to lose their hearts and be damned forever. The head honor guard opened the limo door. Ferruk stepped out first, because that was his honor, then came Honute, Theoris, Akila, Ayruyi and last her father. The hundred guards line snapped to attention and saluted – fist to heart. Honute squinted and saw that the line went all the way to the entrance to the main building. The Sun was high in the sky and it hit Honute full in the face. The warmth stung but felt good.

Inside the main entrance revealed a huge expanse of space and walls. Human body wide columns touched the roof nearly fifty feet high. The air was cool and the lighting low. The floor was polished to the extent that with the low lighting it seemed that one was walking on a glass covered lake. The walls seemed to dance from the reflected light from the floor. Honute nearly bumped into

Ferruk twice. He kept staring at the ceiling, floor, and walls – not necessarily in that order and was impressed with Pharaoh's wealth.

At the far edge of this expanse stood two guards in Anubis customs. Honute heard music play as he approached the guards. The music was deep and touched one at the core of the soul. The beat was at a slow pace. The down stroke seemed to hit every four seconds. The effect was like an amusement park E ticket ride.

Passed the guards a monorail waited. It was polished in gold metal with black silver midlines. It was the size of a large bus and was completely autonomous. Honute geeked and gawked at the marvelous splendor, wonder at the arrangement. Once on board the monorail and the doors shut the ride was smooth. The rail emerged outside and the windows darkened. Honute sat back already exhausted by the moments' events. He looked around and noticed Ferruk and Ayruyi were the only two unimpressed. No doubt Ayruyi had seen this countless times and Ferruk was just putting up a front. He was still amazed how they could remain so poised in all this grandeur. Honute was thinking about that when the monorail turned sharply right, then sharply left - to get everyone's attention, and glided to a halt. The door opened and the great palace filled his view. This was Pharaoh's home. Legend, myth, rumor, and hearsay, all rolled up into one. This was where fantasy met sanity. The complex mix of the fantastic and the mundane and some never got enough. Honute followed everyone out and into the grand hallway, a spit and polish of brown wood panels on the wall and earth-color stone tiles on the floor. Ferruk lead the way in a smaller hallway that seemed to be more fitting for mortals and other lesser beings. The ceiling was still high, twenty feet, and the hallway was still wide, fifty feet, but Honute seemed to like those dimensions. It occurred to him that Pharaoh planned it this way – after being nearly overwhelmed by space and effect one was glad to step into this area.

Ferruk stopped. The group was met by Hydrulia, one of Pharaoh's half sister-wife. She stood as tall as Akila but was leaner and her skin was a shade darker. Her skin was anointed in golden tinted oil and when she talked she seemed to sing the words instead of just saying them. "Welcome, friends, to Pharaoh's house.

Once inside the actual palace Honute could breathe easier. It looked like a palace one would expect. The painted images of gods along the walls and on columns seemed decorative. Under each painting was the name, in hieroglyph – nearly a dead language, of each god and a description of that god's job in the higher order of the universe. Fine woven cloths were hung along the wall with large windows and high vaulted ceilings in every room. The tiles on the floor were smooth and polished to mirror perfection. Guards had been placed at every entrance and only the most senior of officials were allowed in. Hydrulia walked everyone through the offices of Pharaoh, a long stretch way of the different departments of the Blessed Lands. Every single room was dedicated to the comfort of Pharaoh and the Royal family, the thousands of temples through out the Blessed Lands, the civil defense of the Lands, and the collection of money to keep the Pharaoh and his family in comfort. The whole country was here to obey the living embodiment of its gods, from sunrise to sunset and in between. Pharaoh sneezed – the Blessed Lands wiped his nose. Honute took all this in. Every room, every guard, every person and there seemed to be more and more of everything else. At the final stop, the group was met by Drethulia, Pharaoh's first sister-wife. She looked very much like Hydrulia but different. She was older with barely noticeable wisdom lines at the corners of her eyes and lips, but the skin was still smooth and she too was covered in gold tinted oil.

Drethulia said in a very melodic voice, "Our family welcomes you. Please enter." She turned to two tall doors. She spread her arms wide and hummed out a tome that only Honute, Ferruk, and possibly Ayruyi would know.

Hail, O ye who make perfect souls to enter into the House of Osiris, make ye the well-instructed soul of the Osiris the scribe Ani, whose word is true, to enter in and to be with you in the House of Osiris. Let him hear even as ye hear; let him have sight even as ye have sight; let him stand up even as ye stand up; let him take his seat even as ye take your seats.

The great doors opened up to reveal a gang of servants waiting to serve the guest of Pharaoh. Drethulia turned and said that a servant was assigned to each person. She turned to Ayruyi and Arrutyi said, "It has been a long time."

Ayruyi and her father bowed deeply, honored that Pharaoh's first sister-wife acknowledge them. The servants behind Drethulia bowed back.

Ferruk watched intrigued. He had never known this to happen except when servants are being welcomed backed into a home, but since Pharaoh had not told him of this; it must be that Drethulia was being semi-formal. Ayruyi and her father have never been to the palace at the same time.

Drethulia walked up to Honute and bowed.

Honute immediately dropped to his knees and said, "O'mighty Queen Drethulia it is I that should bow to you. I am but a humble servant and priest in the Blessed Lands in service to Pharaoh and the Royal family."

Drethulia lifted Honute up. "Priest Honute, welcome to our home, you have a special place in the palace. Ask any servant for anything as it will be yours."

Honute, stunned, but not enough to forget his manners, bowed his head, "O'mighty Queen, thank you. I shall endeavor to not be a burden on such a magnificent home."

She turned to Ferruk and smiled congenially. "Priest Ferruk, we our most thankful of your bringing Honute and his guest before our home. Pharaoh has heard of the mishap on the rail system. Pharaoh has instructed the BLIA to handle the case —"

Ferruk paled for a moment, but he recovered quickly. He had nothing to worry about, as nothing could or would be traced back to him.

Drethulia continued, "We think that the assassination of the

Royal Oracle and attempt on Priest Honute are related. Be assured justice will be served."

Ferruk swallowed hard and gracefully bowed, "O'mighty Queen, thank you for the welcomed news, with the BLIA on the case I can only imagine the case to be solved." Ferruk thought quickly. His body guard was most efficient and he was positive that suspicion would not fall on him. The Blessed Land Investigative Agency was highly effective at catching criminals and law breakers, but they weren't perfect, as he could attest to that personally.

Drethulia turned to Akila and Theoris. She bowed her head, "Welcome to our home. Pharaoh is grateful of your past deeds and your present results. It is most exciting. Tonight before dinner Pharaoh has granted you an audience." Then she addressed the group. "Please make yourselves at home and allow the servants to help and instruct you wisely. Dinner will be served later tonight after Pharaoh performs the evening ceremony."

Chapter 28

Theoris watched as Pharaoh moved across the room to his chair. She had to admit, he was exquisite looking. His build was just as good as Honute's.

Pharaoh sat down. "Dr. Theoris, make yourself comfortable."

Theoris sat in a chair across from Pharaoh. Theoris thought it odd for a man to have rooms the size of parks he would have his office the size of a broom closet. It, of course, was larger than a broom closet, but going from cathedral sized rooms to an office the size of her's gave Theoris a cramped near claustrophobic feeling.

"May I call you Theoris?"

She nearly tumbled out of her chair. "Mighty Pharaoh? You never have to ask for such a thing."

He laughed, "My dear Theoris, you may relax around me."

Theoris sat with her back flushed to the chair. She tried to slouch, but came off as someone not comfortable with being relaxed.

Pharaoh laughed again. He smiled and pressed a button on his desk.

A moment later a servant walked in with imported wine from the southern province. It was in a white stone pot. The servant poured the clear wine into stone cups. The wine steamed.

Pharaoh said, "It is called Sake. You sip it. It is hot." Theoris did as instructed. She let it touch her lips and she inhaled lightly. It was warm but slipped over her tongue pleasantly. "Quite good." She said.

Pharaoh nodded. "Next week I have a meeting with Nihongo's leader. They don't have Honey wine and we don't have this Sake. I think it's a good start."

Theoris nodded and sipped more of the sake. She was looking forward to seeing it in the stores.

Pharaoh, himself, sipped at his cup. After a moment he put the cup down and sat back. "Theoris, I read your report. It is most enlightening. Particularly the conclusion that Honute may have been the worst candidate for the experiment, emotionally and physiologically. Is he that unstable?"

Theoris thought about the question. "Mighty Pharaoh –"

"Just plain Pharaoh, please."

Theoris almost said just that but instead bowed her head and continued, "Pharaoh, I think he is stable enough. It seems that his powers work on the instinctual level and when he is deeply upset. His conditioning is extraordinary. I can not distinguish between the before and after without carefully asking specific questions. This Honute is the Honute. The old Honute is gone."

"That's your professional opinion?" Pharaoh asked.

Theoris nodded. "It is. I also gut feel it too. I like Honute. He is the humble priest."

Pharaoh thought for a moment then said, "Tonight at dinner I'm going to put your professional opinion to the test."

Theoris gasped. "Pharaoh?"

He smiled.

Under different circumstances she would have swooned.

"Ferruk is going to get a surprise. He will be allowed to strike against me. Would Honute instinctively react to save me?"

Theoris swallowed the rest of the wine and put the cup down. Would he? She was ninety-nine percent certain. She nodded, but that one percent nagged viciously at her gut. "I believe he would try and save you."

Pharaoh laughed. "It's the word 'try' that worries me." And he laughed harder.

Theoris forced hers. It was the word 'try' that worried her as well.

Honute walked into the main dinner room. A huge stone table sat in the middle. Beautifully ornate chairs with carvings of Ma'at, Mut and Bast carved deeply in them surrounded the table. Underneath the table's polished surface lay hand size squares of painted images. Honute read as many as he could see and realized it was Pharaoh's family history. One square outlined the first Cursed Land wars, about 600 years ago, another was a child's poem, probably an original since Honute didn't recognize it. Each square was different and in a way fascinating to read. Pharaoh, himself, assembled the table and it gave an interesting look at the complexities of the man, the living god.

Each place set had a name on it. Pharaoh needed no nameplate. He was at the head of the table. His first-wife on his left, Theoris next to her. There was a place for Arrutyi and Ayruyi - which was very rare. Honute sat immediate right, with Akila next to him. Ferruk was placed at the far end, with Pharaoh's junior wife, Hydrulia. When Ferruk saw that his servants would be eating at the same table as he was did he get perturbed, but when he saw that he was placed at the far end he was insulted. Pharaoh was playing his nerves.

Most of dinner consisted of small chatter. Pharaoh, Akila, Theoris, Drethulia and Hydrulia partook in a liberal amount of wine. Honute sipped. Ayruyi and her father drank water. And Ferruk fumed and passed on most everything. Hydrulia, of course, noticed but did not comment. Ayruyi and Arrutyi noticed as well. Then as the last dinner plate was collected one of the servants brought out a large platter with a top on it. It was placed in front of Ferruk.

Ferruk looked up.

Pharaoh pushed himself away from the table, stood up, and addressed everyone seated. All the servants stood toward the end of the table. "Friends, I'm glad you were able to enjoy the food at my table. The gods have blessed us so well that I thought to share some things with you." He looked at Theoris and said, "Dr. Theoris has again given the Blessed Lands reason to feel safe. Her work, with the help, of her assistant Akila, has demystified some of the unknowns to magick. With her research we can understand and cultivate this fantastic power." Then he turned to Honute, "Our newest family member, Honute. He served us well in the Cursed Land wars, and he will serve us well in our new house." He turned to Arrutyi and Ayruyi. "Our children have come back to use in full circle." Then he turned to Ferruk and said, "Ferruk, it has come to our attention that something is amiss. As it has been for a while but everything was not in the light, as it should have been. I am disappointed. We have given you one of the highest titles of the land and you have abused that privilege."

Ferruk was stunned. Pharaoh had just chastised him in front of everyone.

"Ferruk, when I gave you Arrutyi and Ayruyi my heart was in the grips of pain. I was deeply fond of Ayruyi's mother. When she journeyed over to the underworld it hurt me deeply. And looking into Ayruyi face made me think of her mother. So, with a sad heart I gave them to you because I felt you worthy." Pharaoh sighed heavily and said, "Even one such as I can misjudge strength of character."

Ferruk paled and looked sick to his stomach. His worst nightmare was happening.

Pharaoh said, "I take back what I gave. Arrutyi and Ayruyi are no longer your servants. Honute is now their holder."

Ferruk slammed his fist on the table.

Several guards ran up behind him but Pharaoh told them to stay back. "Lift the cover off the plate."

Ferruk stared with his jaw clenched.

Pharaoh roared at the top of his lungs, "Take the cover off or I will strike you dead."

Ferruk was startled. He fumbled for the cover and yanked it off. It clattered somewhere in the background. Ferruk stared at the contents. All his important papers, documents, and contracts. Printouts of bank statements with areas circled red. And a large knife sat nestled on top. Ferruk looked up to Pharaoh. His eyes puffed and watery.

Everyone on that side of the table got up and moved toward the front.

Pharaoh leaned forward. "The knife is for you, Ferruk. I have voided all your contracts and emptied out your bank account. Your property is mine. You have nothing left but your shame. What are you going to do?"

Tears started streaming down Ferruk's face. He was hit by an uncontrollable fit of tears and couldn't stop. He picked up the knife and pointed the blade at his heart. He looked at each person in the eye and then suddenly flung the blade at Pharaoh.

It was a split second really. Not enough time to even blink, but for Honute it took nearly forever. He saw Ferruk grab the blade and recoil his arm. Then the arm came down and forward and the knife twirled and twisted slowly in the air – it really was a bad throw, but Honute hadn't thought that at the time, just only in retrospect. A foot before the point of the blade rotated down to hit Pharaoh in the face Honute held out his hand. He felt a burning sensation at his finger tips and just as the knife blade touched his hand the metal melted. It and the hilt landed hard on the table.

Ferruk was shocked. To his mind the throw had been perfect. It would have hit Pharaoh in the face, but somehow it didn't. He looked at Honute and for the first time in a while he was afraid. The Oracle's declaration, "He will kill you" resonated in his mind.

Everyone looked at the Pharaoh, the now solid splotch of metal on the table and a wide-eyed Honute.

Pharaoh turned to Honute and said, "High Priest Honute, Vizier of the Middle Regions, Friend of the Royal Family, and the Right hand of Pharaoh, thank you."

The guards hauled Ferruk away.

Honute fainted.

Chapter 29

Ferruk was furious. Pharaoh had stripped him of his titles, in front of everyone. He took away his servants and froze all his assets. He was under a cloud of suspicion and there was talk of criminal charges. He was under house arrest until a formal hearing was convened. And currently the Police Chief and Adjutant General rifled through his belongings. And to make matters worst, Pharaoh gave Ayruyi and her father to Honute. He had to make his own meals and draw his own bath. It was a very embarrassing and compromising position, luckily he could make phone calls.

The first call he made was to his lawyer, the second to a friend who owed him a favor. The third, which took some time, was routed to Pharaoh's temple. An operator who had not heard the news connected him to Ayruyi. While he waited he drank the last of his alcohol. Pharaoh himself gave it to him. It was a fitting present. The drink came from the Cursed Lands. It was fermented with corn and it had a bite.

Ayruyi was soaking in a bathtub. Honute had given her and her father the "day" off. At first she hadn't understood, but when Honute told her to get out and leave him alone she finally got the message. Her father had gotten the idea earlier. He kissed her on the forehead and said "The Gods have heard our prayers." He disappeared into his hotel room. She remembered hearing room service knocking at his door. It was hard at first but after several hours she decided to take a bath and relax. Ten minutes into her bath the phone rang. She jumped out of the tub and dripped water in a beeline to the phone. Her thoughts were that Honute-Ra really did need her. She heard Ferruk's voice and a chill shot up her spine. She froze.

He said, "Ayruyi, it's me, Ferruk. Are you there?"

She remained silent, frozen, scared, and upset.

"Ayruyi? I am worried about you. I miss you?"

Then it finally hit her. She no longer belonged to Ferruk. Broken, weak, foolish, criminal Ferruk. Honute-Ra was her new master and her god. He cared about her and treated her like a person. "May Anubis drop you heart in the river Styx." She said.

Ferruk was silent. He was shocked that Ayruyi would say such a thing. "But Ayruyi, I've never told you this before because I thought it would be inappropriate, but I love you."

A moment passed.

Ferruk said, "Ayruyi, are you there? I need to hear your lovely voice." A few more seconds ticked by, then he heard what sounded like laughter.

Ayruyi couldn't help herself. She started out slowly and before she knew it became hysterical.

Ferruk felt the bottom of his world fall from under him. He slowly placed the receiver in its cradle. Ayruyi's laugh haunted him for a full five minutes. Afterwards, he spat at the phone and cursed her lineage. "I should have given you away when I had the chance." Then he yelled at the phone. "I hate you. You will pay, and pay, and pay. I swear it!"

Ayruyi hung the phone up feeling guilty. For a full five minutes she stood dripping wet staring at the phone. Then she smiled to herself, laughed softly, and walked back into the bathroom to enjoy her bath. She allowed herself the thought, 'Ferruk the fool, Ferruk the clown, Ferruk the idiot, asshole, child.' It all tumbled out in a dizzying wash of emotion. She ran back, soaking wet again, to the phone, picked it up and yelled. "Ferruk, the fucker! I hate you!" She hung the phone up. Then she went back to truly enjoy her bath for she knew who the real master was and who the real slave had been. Ferruk could never have her again.

The Oracle slowly moved across the room and sat heavily in

one of two large upholstered chairs. A small table was nestled between them. A tea pot and two pewter cups sat next to it. "Young Priest Honute, thank you for coming. How are you feeling? Last night was quite a show, was it not?"

Honute stepped through the doorway and looked around. He walked to the Oracle and without asking poured tea into each cup. He looked puzzled, then quietly sat down.

The Oracle laughed sweetly, took a cup and sipped at it. She relaxed and folded herself deeply in the chair. "You don't recognize me, do you?"

Honute searched her face for something recognizable. "Only that you are the Royal Oracle. And that you had been assassinated."

The Oracle laughed. "I am still here thank goodness. It was one of Ferruk's bodyguards who told of the plot. I saw it through my bowl anyway, but decided to give the would-be assassin a chance. I saw good things coming from him. Now to answer that question. We met many years ago. You were but a boy, so young and frail. No one believed you would survive."

Honute said, "Survive?"

The Oracle nodded.

"I was told that as a child I was sick and dying and that there was this . . ." He looked at the Oracle. ". . .woman who saved my life. It was you!"

The Oracle laughed again. She sipped at the tea and smiled broadly. "I love this chair. It is so comfortable."

Honute nodded. He had noticed the chair being very soft. "How?"

The Oracle placed her steely eyes on Honute.

He stared back.

She nodded approvingly. "The conditioning has not left you meek. That is good."

Honute frowned. "Meek? Conditioning?"

"When your father brought you to me I knew you had destiny. You had a rare disease called Neurendodegenerative phalagitis.

One in five hundred million can get it. It is passed on from generation to generation. The last time it was seen was over 2400 years ago. A young boy by the name Tut had a form of it but it was misdiagnosed. We all know the story. He was murdered."

Honute nodded. He knew who King Tut was. Who didn't? But he shared a disease with him? That was different.

"He was never treated. Had he been, we would be worshiping one god." The Oracle chuckled. She reflected as if she had been privy to a private joke. "I treated you when you came to me and here you stand alive and well."

Honute nodded again. He looked at the Oracle and wondered how old she was. She looked ancient. "What did you do to me?"

She laughed. "Nothing."

"Nothing." Honute repeated.

She smiled. "Nothing."

Honute frowned. "Seriously. You're playing with me. You treated me, so it had to be something."

She sipped at the tea and let the liquid languish on her tongue. "Nothing in the sense that I really didn't treat you with medication or some such potent elixir that I let everyone believe. I gave you a neurotoxin." She laughed hard.

Honute nearly dropped his cup. "You meant to kill me?"

"The disease is actually an indicator that something else is happening in your body. The disease is a result of your body trying to change on one level and your body fighting that change on that level. The nerve tissues begin to break down and the outer surface of your muscles and bone begin to deteriorate. Your joint endings in your hand had swelled and if not stopped you would have eventually literally poisoned your own body and gone into cardiac arrest. Very nasty way to die."

Honute nodded.

"What I did was stop your body from fighting the change. The neurotoxin paralyzed you long enough to let the transformation happen."

Honute stared. "Transformation? I don't understand."

"Honute," she said, "you are special. Once in every several generations does something like this happen. Ra, Osiris, Isis, Thoth, Seth, and many before you have once been mortal. They all went through this."

Honute put his cup down. "Thoth? Ra? Isis? Mortal? You are lying! How could you say such things? You are the Royal Oracle, a position of high regards and responsibilities. I can not believe what I am hearing. He dropped down to his knee and with clasped hands said, "Oh, Mighty Thoth, please forgive the Oracle, she must be old and of need of sleep."

The Oracle laughed out loud. She sipped her tea and said. "Honute, young man, please sit back in your chair."

Honute stopped praying and sat. He stared down at his feet and felt doom start to overcome him. What was he to do now? The Oracle told him his gods had once been mortal. But once he started thinking about it, it really didn't make all that difference did it? Pharaoh is the flesh and blood embodiment of Ra and Osiris. He is mortal and will eventually die and he will be replaced.

The Oracle watched Honute's face with interest. He was taking this a little better than she hoped for. Thoth had refused to listen to her for days. It was when she elicited the help of Ma'at did he understand. But back then he was uneducated and a bit stupid. Honute was different though he reminded her of him.

Honute looked up and saw the Oracle looking at him. Her eyes had changed to a lighter shade of brown and the pupils were huge. He quickly looked away.

"Honute, I see you have come to the realization that it doesn't matter how one begins the journey, just how the journey ends."

He kept his head down, but said, "But why are you telling me this?"

"You are going through some changes now, let them happen. I have foreseen your future and it is as it should be."

"I still don't understand?"

His humbled look reminded her of Osiris when she first told him. Seth was a problem. He relished the change and pushed the envelope too quickly. He went nearly mad with jealously and envy of Osiris. "Your journey has begun, Honute. You will never truly be alone. Remember that." She put the cup down and started to get up.

Honute got up and quickly moved to her side to help.

She held his hand as she lifted herself up. "And such a gentleman you are. You are worthy to have the gift. Go now and talk to Akila. You two have much to discuss. Tell her everything, hold nothing back." She stared him in the eyes.

Honute almost flinched, almost.

The Oracle smiled, "Hold nothing back, including your heart."

Honute blushed.

The Oracle walked to one of the doors on the far side of the room and disappeared through the doorway.

Honute walked to the door he stepped through earlier. When he emerged into the hallway Akila was waiting for him. He smiled. "How'd you know to meet me here?"

"One of the Oracle's assistance asked me to wait here. I just got here seconds ago,"

Honute stared at his feet. "We have to talk. I have some things to tell you."

Akila nodded and walked along side of him.

After several minutes they ended up in an open park area. Honute lead Akila to a stone bench and both sat down. He looked her deep in the eyes and smiled. She smiled back. After a moment he said, "Akila, I love you with all my heart and wish for you to be by my side."

Akila beamed and hugged Honute. She kissed him and whispered in his ears, "And I love you too my priest. I love you too."

Chapter 30

Ferruk stared out the window. It was late and he had nothing to do. His phone had been taken away some hours ago, and the AV and radio had been removed as well. Pharaoh meant him to remain locked up in this room in solitude with only his thoughts to keep him company. It was perhaps around three in the morning when he heard the door open. He turned expecting to see one of the guards assigned to him to take something else away, like maybe his pillows or blanket or maybe to short his sheets, something that was designed to make him suffer. Instead, it was someone dressed like a guard. They looked authentic enough, but it was something in their stance that gave him away. Ferruk said, "Yes? Are you here to assassinate me?"

The guard said, "I'm here to help you take revenge."

Ferruk sat up straight and eyed the stranger. "And how will you do that?"

He smiled, "There won't be another guard coming this way for another ten minutes. I'm that favor you asked for."

Ferruk stood up. "How can I trust you?"

"You can't." Then he said, "Look. You tried to kill Pharaoh - that alone should have been the death of you. Before that you embezzled charity funds - that's stealing from Pharaoh's pockets. Another death sentence. You mistreated your servants - that should be a death sentence. You decide, okay. I'm walking away. I won't see you again. Debt paid." The stranger walked out. He left the door opened.

Ferruk stood bewildered. This is what he did not expect. He stepped to the door and looked out. No one. Then he made his way through the hall way to one of the other rooms. Ferruk knew that stealth was not his thing. He wanted to settle some scores but knew it would be foolhardy at best. His best bet was to make his way down to the river edge. He knew from personal experience that guards would leave several vehicles unattended, with keys in the ignition. Ferruk's heart pounded and he sweat profusely. He kept telling himself he could make it, he could make it. He found the room he was looking for. The door was unlocked. He stepped in and made his way to the bedroom. Ayruyi was sleeping soundly. Next to the bed on a night stand was an empty canter of Honey wine. He tip-toed up to her, grabbed and lifted the canter, and hit her on the head with it. The bottle clunked deeply but did not shatter. Her body went slack and her breathing seemed to have stopped. He left the same way he came in, satisfied that he was able to keep at least one promise.

Akila woke up early. She and Honute spent the better part of the late evening making love. She had several orgasms, Honute had two and he was exhausted. So when the evening drifted into the early morning he didn't hear Akila get up. She dressed in a light wrap and walked out onto the grounds. She decided that a nice stroll near the river edge would be nice.

Ferruk made it out the building unobserved. He figured he had a few more minutes to make his escape. He approached the edge of the river, avoiding the camera as best he could, and saw Akila strolling along the river. Revenge number two was in the stars and he ran up behind her. She turned away and he hit her hard in the face. She collapsed in his arms. He tossed her over his shoulders and made it to one of the vehicles. He found one that had the back windows tinted. He threw Akila in the back seat, got in the front seat himself, found the keys in the ignition and drove off. There was a tense moment when one of the guards spotted him on the way out. Ferruk recognized him as the same one who helped him earlier. Ra was looking favorably on him this morning.

181

Honute woke up to commotion outside the door. He dressed in his robe and walked to the door. Outside his room guards hurried everywhere.

Theoris ran up to him. She said, "Akila has been taken by Ferruk."

Honute blinked a few times. "What?" He wasn't sure he heard correctly.

Theoris repeated, "She was taken this morning. One of the cameras caught Ferruk knocking her out and kidnapping her. The BLIA is out looking for them now."

Honute felt a pop deep in his soul. His heart went into tachycardia and a small simmer of rage was forming.

One of the guards yelled out from Ayruyi's room. "Someone get a doctor. The girl is hurt."

Honute ran over to the room and saw Ayruyi's motionless body on the bed. The pillow was soaked in blood, but he heard her faint breathing. He walked over to Ayruyi and placed his warm hand over the wound. A green glow surrounded her head and Honute felt his fingers start to burn. Seconds later the glow disappeared and in the midst of astounded onlookers Ayruyi opened her eyes.

Someone said, "Dear gods, it is true."

Another voice said, "May we all have the strength."

Theoris stood behind Honute and watched. She was pleased.

Suddenly, Arrutyi ran to Ayruyi's side and he cradled her head in his lap. Ayruyi looked at her father and said, "See Father. Honute-Ra saved me. He is a living god." And in a weakened soft voice she chanted, "Honute-Ra, Honute-Ra, Honute-Ra" Then went to sleep.

The doctor ran up to the bed and quickly examined Ayruyi. He scratched his head and said, "There is no wound. It is gone." He then looked at Honute. Everyone did.

Honute looked at his hand.

It started out softly at first but grew louder. "Honute-Ra, Honute-Ra, Honute-Ra" the collective group in the room said. Honute spun toward the group and said, "No, no! I am a humble priest. I am here to serve the people and Pharaoh."

The chant grew louder and louder.

Honute yelled, "Stop. Please stop. I am a simple priest. I am not a god."

But the chanting didn't stop and all the while Pharaoh was standing at the doorway. He moved and the chanting suddenly stopped. The air became thick with uncertainty and uneasiness. Pharaoh walked up to Ayruyi and looked down.

Arrutyi, tears in his eyes, looked into Pharaoh's. "He saved my daughter's life O'mighty Pharaoh."

Suddenly the room stirred and people at the doorway moved. They made way for the Oracle. She walked slowly over to the bed and faced Pharaoh. She stood to the right and behind Honute.

Pharaoh faced the two and the room remained silent. He said, "Honute, you have been given a gift of great power. Do you understand what it means to be a living god?"

Honute shook his head. "O'mighty and great Pharaoh, I just want to be a simple priest who can help people."

Pharaoh touched Honute on the shoulder and Honute bowed his head.

Someone said, "Look, Pharaoh humbles a god. He too is powerful."

"Honute," Pharaoh began, "you are worthy of this gift. May it bring you what it brings you. Come, we found Ferruk and Akila. He is asking for you."

The two walked out.

Ferruk and Akila stood on top of one of Blessed Lands tallest buildings. It was the forward temple of Ra. Ferruk still was running on his favor when he made it to the temple. This was the place he often prayed to Ra during the morning light ceremonies. He, along, with Pharaoh and a handful of assistance had the passkey or knew the passcode to the roof. Once he made it to the roof he made his demand. And now he waited.

The drive to the Temple of Ra took, in Honute's estimation, forever. He thought they would never get there. It was only until the vehicle stopped at the entrance did he think this could be resolved. Police cars, the press and onlookers crowded the area. He stepped out of the car and looked up. The top of the Temple had the eye of Ra looking down upon the Blessed Lands. The eye was carved into a naturally formed quartz the size of a small car. When the Sun's ray passed through the lens the light turned light blue and washed the entire building in its glow. It was awe inspiring. Honute dreamed numerous times to pray to Thoth from atop the building. Now he would pray to Thoth to give him the strength to survive, but if Ferruk asked him to forfeit his life to save Akila's he would gladly and readily do it. So with a sense of foreboding he entered the building, as per instructioned, alone.

Ferruk was growing tired. He had been holding the rifle to Akila's head for nearly an hour. The guard vehicle had been equipped with all sorts of weapons. Ferruk figured that, after this, a new policy would prohibit leaving weapons in unattended vehicles. He thought the guard who did should be shot, but thanked him just as well for giving him a way to leverage the now impending meeting.

The door to the stairs opened and Honute stepped out. He was unarmed and clothed in a simple wrap. Hint of blood was on his sleeve. Ayruyi's he hoped. That ungrateful bitch he thought. He cared for her when she was young and loved her when she got older. He had her learn new and wonderful things and how was he repaid? She laughed in his face. The decanter to the head was a fitting end to her. "Stop right there Honute."

Honute stopped. He was maybe twenty feet from Akila and Ferruk. "Are you okay, Akila?"

She nodded despite the big bruise on her forehead.

Ferruk said, "She is okay, and she will stay that way, if you follow my instructions."

Honute nodded. On the elevator, as it ticked off three hundred floors, he made his peace with Thoth and hoped his death would be swift.

Ferruk smiled and said, "Humble Honute, I am your god and master. My name is Ferruk. You will obey me. There will be no other god you worship but me. Do you understand me?" He finished with a smirk and knew the future was his for the taking. Not long ago he forced Theoris to give Honute hypnotic suggestion. The wording was crucial and she stressed to him that he had to say it that way.

Honute heard Ferruk say something but he couldn't wrap his mind around the words. They sounded garbled and like meaningless noises. But they were familiar and he knew they had meaning. It was after Ferruk uttered the words did he remember that something he forgot he had to do. He blinked.

Ferruk looked at the motionless Honute. "I am your god and you will worship only me. Do you understand?"

Honute's face went slack and his eyes became glossy. A slight tint of blue formed around his hands.

Ferruk frowned. Honute should have bowed to him and declared him as his god. Then it dawned on him that Theoris had made a mistake. Then he grasped that she did not make a mistake. She tricked him. And as Honute's hands glowed brighter and brighter he remembered the Oracle's prediction: "Head Priest of the Middle Lands, Vizier of the Area for Pharaoh, Friend to the Royal Family, he will kill you." The old bag, curse her, would be right. He stepped back toward the edge, dragging Akila with him. Honute stepped toward him, hands bright blue and eyes blazing blue. His face was twisted up into a ravenous expression. "Stop Honute, stop!"

Honute stepped closer. Something made him walk toward Ferruk.

Ferruk yelled, "I will kill her if you come any closer!"

Honute kept coming.

Ferruk realized that Theoris made it so that Honute would not stop. He looked over the edge and saw all the people below him.

He thought 'The sick bastards are hoping blood is shed.' Then an aerocopter flew over head and hovered just off to the side. Ferruk smiled to himself as he noted the "news" symbol stenciled on the side of it. Up close and personal the people wanted news. And at that moment Ferruk made up his mind. He would deny Honute the opportunity to kill him and thus void the Oracle's prediction. He stepped closer to the edge and balanced himself and Akila on the ledge. He whispered in her ear. "I will see you by the river Styx."

Akila said, "What?" and then she felt herself pulled off the edge. Ferruk took a powerful leap dragging Akila with him.

Theoris arrived to the Temple with Pharaoh and the Oracle. She told them that Ferruk had forced her to reprogram Honute to obey him. She admitted that she sabotaged the suggestion and said that Honute would turn on Ferruk. Once Honute had turned he wouldn't stop until Ferruk was dead. She felt smug with herself until she heard someone yell "Mighty gods, he jumped! And he took the girl with him!" She looked up and saw two bodies move away from the building. It was a nightmare.

Honute remembered Ferruk saying something about he would kill someone. It didn't make any sense to him. He thought, 'Who are you going to kill?' Then he felt himself run to the edge of the building and jump. He saw sky and smoke and splashes of random images but nothing he could coherently put together. The world was a jumbled mix of pictures, sounds and sensations and it made him dizzy.

Ferruk tossed the rifle away as he pulled Akila with him. He had a sick perverse feeling of satisfaction that he picked his own demise. He wandered if he would feel the ground hit him or if he would pass out first. Then he looked at the edge of the building and saw Honute leap off after them. Honute come up fast and snatched Akila out of his grip. Ferruk looked behind him and realized the ground would come up soon enough. He felt a burning sensation tug at his skin and felt his eyebrows pucker up and burn away. He looked at the floating image of Honute staring down at him, the very same image from the Oracle's bowl. Then he saw the bright blue blinding burst of light. The heat was intense and brief. He felt the searing air choke deep in his throat as he tried to inhale. Something knotted up tightly in his throat and then release. A rush of cold air to his chest made him panic as he realized his throat was gone. Then he felt something solid hit him in the back of his head.

Theoris watched, as everyone else did, with a mixed feeling of fear and awe. She watched Ferruk's out stretched body being envelope in a bright blue light. Piece of clothing flew off and it looked like his flesh was being ripped off as well. Then he hit the ground, hard. The body smacked loudly and embedded itself deep in the ground. Seconds later a Honute with a limp Akila in his arms floated to the ground. The ground below him seemed to boil and it broke up into tiny pieces of rumble. When his feet touched the ground the blue glow vanished and his eyes returned to normal. He collapsed exhausted and unconscious. The crowd approached cautiously and formed a circle. A few seconds later Pharaoh came up beside Honute and felt at his neck for a pulse. He pointed to an onlooker, a teenager, and then pointed to Akila. The teenager, shocked and stunned, walked himself to Akila and lifted her up. Pharaoh picked up Honute in his arms and both walked toward a gang of medical personnel rushing to them. The Oracle followed behind the four. Theoris followed behind her.

Epilogue

Hypatia approached Honute and Akila. A Peace Officer of the Royal Guards was at her side. When she was close enough to be heard she stopped and said, "Officer, that woman has been having an affair with my husband. I want her arrested."

Honute, shocked, looked at Hypatia. "What are you doing?"

Hypatia looked Honute in the eyes, "I'm getting you back. This . . . this" Her hand shaking as she pointed, "this bitch has cast a spell on you. She has poisoned your mind with lies."

Honute moved Akila behind him. "She has not poisoned my mind. All that she says has been true."

Hypatia said, "You are still my husband and I invoke the old laws. This witch must pay for her crime."

Honute frowned and he felt himself get warm. "She is not a witch Hyp. I love her . . . "

Hypatia threw her hands to her ears. "Lies, all lies. She is a witch and must be dealt with accordingly. Officer, it is your duty."

The Peace Officer drew his gun and pointed it toward the ground. "Miss, please come with me."

Honute shifted his weight toward the Officer. "Please, Officer, there is a misunderstanding. This is all a mistake."

"I am sorry, Priest Honute. The law is the law."

Hypatia puffed her chest out as if in triumph.

Honute squared off in front of both of them. His feeling of betrayal turned into anger and he became hot. "If you are invoking the old law then I will answer you in the old law."

Hypatia's smile faded. "What do you mean?"

Honute said. "I, Honute, Priest of the Temple of Thoth invoke the old law of marriage. As Priest of the old ways it is my right . . ."

Hypatia realized what Honute was doing. Her voice raised an octave higher then normal. "Honute, you mustn't do this. I still love you."

Honute continued, ". . . it is my right to follow the laws of our forbearers, it is my right to bring witness all those around us."

"No!" She said.

Honute said with clenched teeth, "I divorce you. I divorce you."

Hypatia screamed, "No, you can not do this!"

Honute looked her in the eyes. "I am giving you want you wanted. You left me. You asked for this. I am giving it to you."

"No! No! No! You can not."

"I divorce you!"

Hypatia's scream filled the air in an earsplitting tone. She collapsed to her knees and sobbed uncontrollably.

The Peace Office placed his gun back in the holster and straightened up. He looked down at Hypatia and reached a hand out to console her.

She wailed loudly. After a few moments she looked up and wiped her tears away.

Honute and Akila turned to leave.

"Stop!" Hypatia said and grabbed the Peace Officer's gun. She stepped away and aimed it at Akila.

Honute turned and said, "Hyp, it's over. You finally got what you wanted."

"No!" She yelled. "What I wanted was a husband who had a backbone. I wanted a man and not some boy complacent in doing minion work. I wanted you to be that man. You had it within you to become Vizier and High Priest. But instead you had settled for some damned statue washer. Now you are to be Vizier. It is not fair I say! Not fair at all!"

Honute took a step forward. "Please Hypatia, let me go. I was never those things and you know it. It is not your fault. Please. Let's walk away."

"No! Never!" And she squeezed the trigger.

Honute yelled, "No!" and heard the click of the mechanism

inside the gun. He felt a pop deep inside his head and everything around him seemed to move in slow motion. He saw smoke slowly puff out the gun and heard a muffled "bang!" The bullet slowly peeked out the barrel and moved in inches. Honute turned and stepped toward Akila. He reached her and moved her a foot away from the bullet. He stepped back into the place he had been standing in when the gun went off. He felt another deep pop inside him and the world snapped back into real-time.

The bullet sparked off the wall and ricocheted elsewhere.

The Peace Officer reached out and snatched the gun from Hypatia.

Akila had lost her balance and fell bumping her head slightly on the concrete. She got up and touched her body for an entry point. None.

Hypatia looked on in amazement. For a second she thought she saw Honute's image blur. She squeezed her eyes tight and shook her head.

The Peace Office looked closely and noted that Akila had not been shot. His years of experience told him otherwise but the proof was before him. The young woman escaped death, bless the goddess Mut. Maybe the rumors are true. Maybe this humble priest is truly powerful. After the incident at the Temple of Ra, Pharaoh had declared a news blackout. He saw the footage before the blackout but thought it to be special effects. It looked real enough, but who could do what the AV showed.

Honute turned and helped Akila up. He looked at Hypatia, who was now handcuffed. He shook his head as the Peace Officer dragged her away. Hypatia screamed, kicked, and yelled obscenities as she was led away. He made a mental note to see if he could help her out. The law is pretty harsh with those who attempt murder.

Epilogue II

Inside was the new High Priest. The Vizier of the Middle Regions of the Blessed Lands, Friend of the Royal Family, Right Hand and Instrument of Pharaoh, Honute Carael-Ra. Outside stood a million curious citizens, waiting. The air was thick with drizzle and anticipation. It hung silent like all those present. In a few minutes, the long awaited question would be answered. Who was Honute Carael-Ra, the unknown humble priest with Magickal powers? Was he a servant of Pharaoh, or a new deity destined for wondrous things?

Akila fussed over Honute. She made sure that his robe looked impeccable.

"Akila," Honute protested over the attention. "I feel silly wearing this thing. I don't see why I can't sit on the seat in my regular clothing."

Akila brushed at the material. It was a spun gold polymer with silver metal trimming. It was deceivingly heavy, hot, and restrictive. She brushed at the shoulders and they seemed to radiate a brighter yellow-orange color than the rest of the robe. She rubbed her hand down the length of the entire robe and it radiated brightly. Akila stepped back and smiled. "That is better."

Honute stood still pouting, waiting for her to finish.

Akila stepped close to Honute, placed a hand on his cheek, and gave him a tender kiss on the lips. "You look just wonderful."

Honute couldn't help himself, he smiled. Akila seemed to make his heart sing just with a few words and the right touch. Thoth he loved her so. He whispered a quick prayer to Isis and thanked her.

Akila asked, "What was that for?"

His smiled widened. "It was a prayer to Isis. I thanked her for bringing you into my life."

Akila blushed and smiled. She wiped the corners of his mouth off, making sure lipstick didn't show. The new High Priest could not be seen with someone else's lipstick on. Akila fought Honute on putting his face together. Finally he settled on a light blush for his cheeks and a clear gloss for his lips. She stepped back. "The people are waiting for you."

Ayruyi stood in the corner and smiled. Honute-Ra was going to take his place in history. And she was going to be a part of it.

He nodded and stepped out the chamber. Only weeks ago he would have never believed he would be worthy enough to walk the halls of the Temple of Ra, in the main capitol. The week before Pharaoh himself welcomed Honute, Akila, his sister Honuti, Ayruyi, her father and Theoris to his dinner table. He was still jazzed from that.

The stone passageway stretched out in front of him. It might have been a hundred miles for all that Honute felt. Like the other countless High Priest before him he had to walk the passageway alone - in silence. With only the thoughts in his head, true or false, only he, Pharaoh, the Gods and the Oracle would know. May Thoth have mercy on his soul.

"I have not done falsehood against men, I have not impoverished my associates, I have done no wrong in the Place of Truth, I have not learned that which is not, I have done no evil, I have not made daily labor in excess of what was to be done for me, my name has not reached the offices of those who control slaves, I have not deprived the orphan of his property, I have not done what the gods detest, I have not slandered a servant to his master, I have not caused pain, I have not made hungry, I have not made to weep, I have not killed, I have not turned anyone over to a killer, I have not caused anyone's suffering, I have not diminished the food-offerings in the temples, I have not debased the offering cakes of the gods. I am Honute, a simple priest who humbly walks the passage way of the High Priest. I give unto you Thoth my essence and my life. I give unto

you that which makes me the penitent entity I am. I am your servant, to command. I am your servant from the beginning to the very end. From eternity to that of judgment Thoth, oh great God of gods, your house will rise above all. I declare it so."

And, thus the crowd saw Honute-Ra, Vizier of the Middle Regions of the Blessed Lands, Friend of the Royal Family, Right Hand and Instrument of Pharaoh, and would-be new god.

The End

ABOUT THE AUTHOR

Born and raised in Southern California, J Carrell Jones has worked in the Customer Support field (private and Government) for over 30 years. His current position as a Technical Support Manager for a Digital Telephone Service Provider allows him to feed the family and pay some bills. He is an Army Veteran, where he worked in Computer Operations – last active duty mission served was for Project Restore Hope. Currently, he lives in Inglewood, California with his wife, a beautiful daughter, a female cat named Perilous and a dozen fish.